# MY MARILYN

### A NOVEL

# ART JOHNSON

STORY MERCHANT BOOKS
LOS ANGELES
2018

STORY MERCHANT BOOKS

Story Merchant Books
400 S. Burnside Avenue #11B
Los Angeles, CA 90036

www.storymerchantbooks.com

ISBN: 978-1-7323411-0-4

Cover Design by Claire Moore
Interior Design by Indie Designz

# Also by Art Johnson

*Seven Visions and Other Poems*

*The Devil's Violin*

*Deadly Impressions*

# FROM ART JOHNSON'S READERS:

"Art Johnson's intrigue and suspense is off the charts!"
—*Melanie Adkins, Amazon Top 500 Reviewer*

"Art Johnson is a master of at least two worlds…that of fiction writing and of music history. Just the best kind of book."
—*Author Tom Stern, M.D.*

"If you like tightly written novels full of intrigue and mystery, this book is for you!"
—*Patricia Statham, Amazon Top Reviewer*

"What a powerful and thrilling mystery!"
—*Zone Critic*

"This is a very clever and enjoyable story. It would be worth your while to read it. Very interesting and entertaining."
—*Jack Great Game, Amazon Top 500 Reviewer*

"Author Art Johnson has a clean, direct, and to-the-point style of writing. A quick, entertaining read, *The Devi's Violin* will keep you guessing."
—*Terrylynn, Amazon Top 500 Reviewer*

*For Philippe Rahmy-Wolff,*

*in fond memory of days spent dreaming.*

# Author's Preface

The cultural and historical significance of Marilyn Monroe needs no introduction. This book came to be because the author has carried with him, for many decades, a concept of the film star away from the silver screen.

As my previous novels utilize real historical events to launch a fictional tale, this book is built with the same construction; familiar names and places mixed with elements plucked from the clouds.

The locations in Los Angeles are a mixture of actual places and the author's whimsy. Having lived and worked in the city of angels for twenty years, my imagination took me back to familiar haunts and characters that left an impression on me.

I am a storyteller, and this is my story about her: fact passed off as fiction, and fiction passed off as fact—a synthesis of Hollywood.

Art Johnson
Monaco
2018

# Chapter 1

*Los Angeles*
*Monday, June 4th, 1962*
*8:15 a.m.*

"Fuck poetry!"

Allan Weisman was enraged. Seated at his desk, the person I'd hoped would be my new boss slammed his fist down on the blue-inked ferrotyped copy of my first submitted article: a review of Carl Sandburg's collected poems. The managing editor leaned back in his chair, rubbed his eyes, and ran his fingers slowly down the length of his face. His tirade was non-stop.

I was on the receiving end—a lanky twenty-five-year-old recently added to the staff of the Los Angeles *Herald Examiner*.

"Listen kid, I hired you on the recommendation of Syd Gould, who told me, with great enthusiasm, that you were a gifted story hound. What is this poetry review bullshit? I already have a cultural writer on staff who drives me nuts with his lengthy articles about theater openings, which I have to personally cut down by fifty percent because the idiot doesn't have the slightest clue on how to self-edit. He's my wife's nephew, and if he wasn't, he'd be out on his ass."

I felt like an actor in a surrealistic play. This was my first official day with the paper. I tried to calculate how fast I could pack up my newly assigned desk and be out the front door.

Weisman continued to rant, "What the hell is your name?"

I pointed to the by-line on the review.

Weisman glanced down. "Okay, Rory Long, let me tell you something, in case you missed out on the latest developments on planet earth in the past year or so. This is nineteen sixty-two. None of our readers could give a shit about an old man sitting in a rocking chair, somewhere in Connecticut, making up verses about the wind-blown boughs of pine trees while all the little forest creatures frolic about."

The stale stench of cigarette butts filled the office. I guessed Weisman to be a three-pack-a-day man.

He was on the warpath. "We've got a fucking Catholic for President, while Khrushchev and his Russian cronies are dying to stick a nuclear missile up our ass."

He paused to make sure he had my attention,

"Some information about where that's headed is what we need to keep everyone in this building looking forward to a paycheck at the end of each week."

The boss lit his third cigarette in the past ten minutes. He shook his free index finger at me.

"And if, by chance, you're not getting the point, then just grab an empty box, fill it up with everything you've put in, or on your desk, and take a hike."

I took his tongue lashing without folding.

Actually, I wasn't surprised. I had expected something like this while finishing the article at six a.m. on the dining room table in my apartment in Silver Lake. I was confident, at this point, that my new boss was unaware of my ace in the hole. It didn't really matter. I may as well go down in a blaze of cannon fodder.

If I were fired on the spot, I'd have the satisfaction of setting a new world record for the shortest career in the newspaper game.

Weisman paused, looking me up and down. I must have been a sight. My crop of disheveled, curly black locks uncombed, mounted on a head with a brow too big for my face, standing six feet tall, weighing only one hundred and thirty-five pounds.

"Well, I'm waiting. Do you have anything to say before I throw this horseshit review of yours in the trash, and you along with it?"

I shot a smile that put him on alert. "Well, Mr. Weisman, would I be correct in assuming that, in your opinion, anyone in the newspaper business takes on the responsibility to be aware of current events on a daily basis?"

He lit his fourth cigarette without responding. He wasn't sure where this was going, but his curiosity was gaining ground. He shrugged.

I continued, "Well then, I would assume that you spend a portion of each day thumbing through weekly periodicals such as *The Saturday Evening Post*,

*Life, Reader's Digest, Look, Time,* as well as *Collier's,* just to keep up on national and international affairs?"

Weisman was losing his patience. "Look, kid, I haven't got the time…"

I cut him off and tossed the most recent issue of *Life* magazine onto his desk.

The veteran newsman glanced at the cover: a full page, black-and-white photo of a dreamy-eyed Marilyn Monroe seated at the feet of Carl Sandburg, in his farm house in Connecticut, staring up at him.

I jumped in before Weisman had a chance to respond. "This just hit the streets at three a.m. I was out taking a walk—couldn't sleep. I grabbed a copy and went to the all-night bookstore on Ninth and Wall to pick up the new edition of Sandburg's poems. When I got back home, I read for a while to capture his mood, then spent the rest of the night and early this morning writing this review.

"The photo is a shocker. I don't think there are many fans out there who believe she has enough brain power to read a book, let alone sit at the feet of America's premier poetic voice in adoration.

"It made sense to me that the rival papers would also follow up. I was trying to scoop the competition by having this ready for the afternoon edition." I lit a cigarette, brandishing a big smile. "As soon as this issue of *Life* hits the streets, I'm confident the cover will be the talk of the town. So, you see, Mr. Weisman," I flicked an ash that missed the editor's ashtray by a mile, landing on his desk-blotter. I didn't flinch. "I wanted to submit a pertinent article, so that we can, as you just stated, all look forward to a paycheck next week."

Weisman stared at me expressionless. Without saying a word, he hit a switch on his call-box.

"Yeah, Carol, tell Brown to get up to my office on the double. I've got an article here that has to make the afternoon edition. We're going to print in less than an hour."

Weisman folded his hands in front of him, nodding his head up and down. "Okay kid, you win this round, but from now on try to get a story off the street that has something to do with crime, politics, sex, or drugs." Weisman brushed away my errant cigarette ash without comment. "That shouldn't be too hard an assignment for a go-getter like yourself, since it's hard to define the difference between the aforementioned categories." We both smiled. Weisman lit his fifth cigarette.

"…Go get some breakfast, you look like shit. Take a nap and report back to me at one o'clock. I'll have an assignment for you then."

I bowed while walking backwards and exited.

Alone in his office, the stunned editor gave the new reporter's review a thorough going-over. It appeared to have all of the qualifications: it was intelligently written without distancing the average reader; precise and to the point. There weren't any snooty, literary ego phrases. "Just the facts, ma'am," as Jack Webb told his audience every week on television's *Dragnet*.

The kid tied in the *Life* cover photo at the beginning of the piece, and, true to word, as the magazine would not be on the streets much before the afternoon edition of the *Examiner*, this article would be a scoop on rival papers.

Weisman pictured his competitor, Syd Gould at the *Herald Tribune*, chewing on his endless cigar and calling his golfing buddy a son-of-a-bitch as he read the review.

A knock at the door. "Yeah, come in."

It was Carol Thompson, Allan's girl Friday, secretary, unofficial psychologist, and dear friend for over ten years. In a rare occasion of close working relationships, their friendship had never sprouted a sexual gesture. They both liked and respected each other for what they had to offer to the daily grind.

"Tom asked me to bring the article down to him. He's swamped with trying to finish setting the San Fernando Valley's water dispute editorial your lordship commanded to be ready for print before the sun rises." She made a comical, theatrical gesture, normally met by her boss with a grin. No response. Carol realized he wasn't paying attention. He was deep in thought.

"What's up, Chief?"

Weisman came back to earth. "This article gets precedence over the editorial. Have Brown place it in column two, page two, and get back to me as soon as he's finished. This has to be in the afternoon edition."

Carol couldn't believe her ears. She snatched up the review and began to read. "Who is Rory Long?"

Weisman took a deep breath. "He's that kid Syd recommended to me a couple of weeks ago."

Carol read moving her lips. "Is this true? The cover of this week's *Life* has a picture of Mrs. Tits and Ass cuddling up with Mr. Everyman's poet?"

Allan tossed Carol the copy of *Life* Rory had given him.

She let out a sigh. "Wheeeew…who da' thunk it?"

Weisman rubbed his hands together. "Well I'll tell you one thing, my dear, this is going to make some heads roll. Even that bastard Walter Winchell is going to have to eat some shit. Everyone believes that Monroe is just another dizzy blonde. When the kid's review hits the streets, exposing Monroe's love of great literature, a fresh take on her will hit the streets, and we'll be first in line to follow up. I should have known that her relationship with Arthur Miller was more than a fling. She's a goddamn closet intellectual." Weisman clapped his hands together. "Oh, boy, this is going to be fun."

Carol sat down and concentrated in silence as she reread the review. "This kid's only been on the paper one day, and he comes up with this?" She stood up ready to head downstairs.

"Did you give him a raise, or what?"

Weisman burst out laughing. "No, as a matter of fact, I chewed him out on the carpet and damn near fired him for wasting the paper's time and money."

Carol scoffed. "Oh…great. Mr. Insightful strikes again! I hope to hell he isn't packing up his desk to head out for another paper. If this article is any indication, this kid's got what it takes."

Weisman leaned back in his chair with his hands clasped behind his head, sporting a huge grin. "Right now, I believe our budding genius is finishing his pancakes and eggs downstairs at Woolworth's counter and will soon be returning to take a well-deserved nap in our coffee room."

The boss of the number one newspaper in Los Angeles bolted upright in his chair. "Hey, maybe I'll go set out a blanket and pillow for him."

Carol opened the door and glanced back. "I've got it chief; one blanket and pillow coming up."

I strode into the newsroom just after nine a.m. having wolfed-down my breakfast. There was a woman waiting for me at my desk.

"What's with you, kid? No pictures of family or even your favorite pet to relieve you from the trap you've gotten yourself into by working here?"

I rolled a toothpick around in my mouth. "Hey, I'm only twenty-five, not a lot of life behind me to display in neat little frames." I winked. "I'm Rory Long."

She smiled. "… Carol Thompson, and I've probably been around here for too many years, but if I'm right, and I usually am, I think you've got a future as a journalist."

She shook my hand. "How was your pancakes and eggs?"

"I had waffles and sausages."

"Mazel tov. Come with me." She crooked her finger. We wound our way along a maze of desks arriving at a small office with frosted-windows. Inside it reeked of stale coffee.

"In case no one told you, the door to the right in this godforsaken rabbit hutch leads to a smaller room with two couches, generally utilized by the late night crew for a brief nap or…you, know."

I nodded.

Carol paused by the door. "I'll wake you up around eleven-thirty so you can grab a bite before your meeting with his highness." Carol was forty-two and had never been married to anyone or anything, except her job. "Catch a few Zzz's." She closed the door softly.

I sat on the couch kneading the down-feathered pillow. My eyes traced the elaborate design of the hand-quilted comforter. I loosened my tie and took off my shoes. I'd been up for nearly twenty-four straight hours.

At one o'clock sharp, I found myself standing on the same spot in front of Allan Weisman's desk as I had that morning. He was on the phone. He held his index finger in the air: the international sign for, *I'll be right with you.*

I glanced around his office. There were several black-and-white, framed photos of Weisman with some of Hollywood's legends. One showed Weisman and Cary Grant laughing their asses off about something. Another showed him in a concentrated pose, listening intently to Alfred Hitchcock. But most impressive were two color shots: one with former President Dwight D. Eisenhower, the other with the man just before Ike, Harry S. Truman. Both shots were taken on a golf course, each man holding his club of choice.

Weisman hung up. "Have a seat, kiddo." The editor lit up another coffin nail. "Try one of mine?"

I shook my head.

"You don't waste words, do you, son? I like that about you, but I'm afraid you and I are going to need more than sign language from now on." As Weisman finished his sentence, he reached behind his chair and hefted a cardboard box full of file folders. He plopped the box onto the desk. It made a heavy thud.

"Okay, my friend, here's where it's at." Weisman dropped his cigarette into the ash tray but let it burn. "As I'm sure you are aware, from your studies in college…"

I detected a hint of sarcasm in his delivery.

"…every major newspaper in America has a dead file that needs to be revisited, from time to time, to try and get another story angle out of some crime or tragedy which has remained unresolved over the years."

I exhaled slowly.

Weisman smiled. "That's right, my friend, it's the same as the cops. The new guys or gals get the privilege of shouting that great Count Basie line—one more time." He dumped the contents of the box onto his desk. "You are going to deliver to me a two column article on the unsolved case of the Black Dahlia." Weisman rubbed his hands together with glee.

"Now, just in case you are completely unfamiliar with this baffling murder of a waitress who had hopes of becoming a Hollywood star, all the details are in these folders."

My expression told it all. I sifted through the stack of eight bulging file folders. There was a mixture of newspaper articles, handwritten notes in pencil and ink, copies of police reports, witness testimony, typed summations and speculations, as well as brown-with-age photos of the murder scene, the victim, and the blood and gore of it all. I paused and looked at Weisman.

"…And you want this by…?"

Weisman pointed to a day on his wall calendar. "Would Saturday next be too much to ask?"

I placed the folders back in the box and stood. "Well, if that's the case, I'd better get a move on it. Is there anything else?"

My new boss moved around from the back of his desk and placed his hand on my shoulder.

"Look, kid, I know you're thinking that this is some kind of punishment, but it isn't. It's a right-of-passage in this business. Everyone goes through it, even yours truly."

I was trying to imagine the man standing before me with yellow, nicotine stained teeth, now in his mid-forties, and what he must have looked like when he was my age. "Is it fair to ask you, who gave you your first assignment?"

Weisman glanced at his rogue's gallery of photos. He stared at one of Edward R. Murrow and himself, both in army uniforms, London Fog overcoats and helmets. "It was Murrow; we were in France, covering the end of the war. He gave me a box very similar to the one you're leaving with. The story I had to come up with was a new angle on Auschwitz."

His turned to me and rolled his eyes. "A real barrel of laughs, that one."

# Chapter 2

I returned to my desk, stacked the files on top, and began to pore through them while sipping on a *Dad's Old -fashioned* root beer. I went through the *Examiner's* summary case-book on the Black Dahlia, checking it against police reports.

Glancing through folders, it dawned on me that I was working alongside veteran reporters, each busy with their own assignments. When I occasionally looked up, there was a smile or a nod coming from one of the others. It was just like being in a Frank Capra movie. Somehow, I had managed to score a touch-down in my first game as a freshman quarterback.

Beneath the file folders, the afternoon edition of the *Examiner* was opened to my review. While researching, I would occasionally look at my article in disbelief. It was amazing to see myself in print with a by-line in bold type. I owed it all to another sleepless night. My chronic insomnia finally payed off.

I paused to think about Weisman in France, covering the war with Murrow. Wow, things sure happen fast in this business. Two weeks ago I wasn't sure if I would be able to find a job. Today, I was a newspaper man.

The afternoon went by swiftly.

At six o'clock, it was time to punch out and head for dinner and home. For the married reporters, it was home and dinner. I decided to give myself a treat and dine at the Brown Derby on Wilshire Boulevard. I had put together a small folder of items from the case to take with me. As I put on my coat and hat and pushed my chair in, the phone rang. It was five minutes after six. I looked over at the switchboard. The operator was making sign language. I picked up.

The operator spoke seven magical words. "Marilyn Monroe on line two, for you."

I gave her a blank stare. She shrugged her shoulders. Was this a joke, kind of a cub reporter's initiation, staged by my colleagues? Whatever it was, I'd better take the call so I could go to dinner. I was starving. "Hello, this is Rory Long, what can I do for you?"

My heart froze as that unmistakable purring, velvety voice said shyly, "Mr. Long…? This is Marilyn Monroe, have I caught you at bad time?"

My insides began to go on a roller coaster ride, acting out a piece of patented humor utilized by the Three Stooges: hommina …hommina … hommina…, that stammering nervous, I-don't-believe-this-is-happening reaction.

The goddess of cinema queried, "Mr. Long, are you there?"

I cleared my throat. "Yes, Miss Monroe, I think I'm still here."

She giggled in that sexy, subdued way. "Well, I'm not trying to scare you, Mr. Long."

I could see a few stragglers had gathered around the operator's booth. They stared through the thick window that separated it from the noisy newsroom. I turned away from the onlookers and sat down. My knees were weak.

"Geez, Miss Monroe, this is indeed an honor; I mean…is there something I can do for you, or…?"

"Oh, I just wanted to tell you how much I enjoyed your review of Carl's poetry. You're the first person that I've come across who I believe has captured the feeling of Mr. Sandburg's poems, *Chicago* and *Skyscrapers*. I felt obligated to tell you how I felt."

I was speechless. 'Well, I'm beside myself, Miss Monroe."

She shot back, "My friends call me Marilyn."

I almost passed out. "And mine call me Rory." I couldn't believe I'd just said that to *her*.

She giggled. "Actually, I was expecting someone older, you sound so young. How old are you, Rory?"

I answered nervously, "I'm twenty-five, but I'm getting older."

Marilyn chuckled. "Well, don't rush it, it happens soon enough, believe me."

I didn't have a response. She continued. "Do you have a pencil and paper handy?"

I fumbled with my desk drawer. "Yes, ma'am, ready to go."

Marilyn giggled again. "Wow, I'm not sure anyone has ever called me ma'am; it makes me feel quite old."

I slapped my face and thought, Jesus, what a fucking idiot. "Sorry, Miss Monroe, I mean, Marilyn. I didn't mean to offend you, I just…"

She cut in. "Forget about it Rory, it just struck me funny. Take down this phone number, if you will."

I pressed so hard on the pencil that I broke the lead. I grabbed a pen.

She continued. "Could you give me a call in the morning, say, around ten o'clock? I'd like to talk to you about something. I need to think it through tonight. Is that alright with you?"

I replied, "Yes, ma'am…I mean Marilyn, I'll call you at ten sharp."

"Goodnight Rory." The phone went dead. A round of applause burst out from the switch board. I waved at the group and headed for the exit. I now believed I more than deserved dinner at the Derby.

I ordered a steak medium rare with a baked potato, green peas, and a glass of wine. The restaurant was packed that night, and although Clifton Webb and Gary Moore were dining two booths away from me, I hardly noticed. My mind was boggled.

I breezed through dinner, hardly tasting anything. I left half of my chocolate marble, three layer cake on the plate, paid at the front counter, and caught the bus back to my apartment. I relived the phone call from the star over and over in my head.

Once home, I tossed the Black Dahlia folder onto my dining-room table and plopped down on the couch. I pulled out the wadded-up piece of paper I had scribbled Marilyn's phone number on and stared at it.

It was now after ten o'clock. In twelve hours I would be talking with every man's fantasy. Was my review of Sandburg's poetry that insightful? I'd read it so many times I could recite it by heart.

I was exhausted but not tired. I took another peek at the Dahlia folder. A dead file: the unsolved murder which took place in nineteen-forty-seven. The crime was nearly fifteen years old. I glanced through the material in an attempt to keep my mind off Marilyn. For the first time since the sun went down, I yawned. It had been a long first day on the job.

When I passed my bookcase, heading for bed, the spine of Edward R. Murrow's autobiography caught my attention. My mother had given it to me for my last birthday. I hadn't read it yet. Standing by the bay window of my Bronson Avenue apartment, I flipped the pages to the glossary, reading by the yellow light cast from a street lamp. I found Weisman's name and turned to page one-ninety-seven.

Murrow described an incident that occurred in London at the close of the Second World War. Weisman was mentioned as a witness to the event without much detail.

That's real life, isn't it?

Men go to battle and bring home their own souvenirs of the fight.

I replaced the book and stared at the subdued, yellow glow of the streetlamp. I couldn't turn my brain off. I tried to make sense of the day. It started by almost getting the ax, and ended up with a call from Marilyn Monroe. Okay, I wrote a pretty good review which impressed the most talked about woman on the face of the planet. So…what does she want?

Finally in bed, I listened on my crystal radio to a broadcast of Alvino Rey's orchestra, coming direct from a ballroom in Albuquerque, New Mexico. The bandleader's steel guitar sounded liked melodic ocean waves.

Soon, I was asleep in the deep.

# Chapter 3

When Swiss-born Willard Waggenstef took his first steps on Ellis Island at the close of World War II, he felt he was finally home. During the war years he'd learned about the restaurant and hotel business in his hometown of Lausanne, shielded from the violent and bloody conflict by his neutral place of birth. He had one goal in mind during this horrid period: to immigrate to America as soon as possible.

The small, rotund man with an engaging smile arrived in New York, penniless, but soon sized up the chances of finding work. He began in small restaurants and delicatessens, doing anything from washing dishes to serving and bartending.

It didn't take long for his employers to recognize his Swiss dedication to detail, as well as his ability to anticipate the needs of those he served. He advanced through the ranks quickly to jobs uptown.

He was made the manager of the St. Moritz Hotel's prestigious dining room, facing the west side of Central Park, when he was only thirty years old. Normally, a position of such prestige was reserved for more mature and experienced persons.

In the process of catering to the elite in upper Manhattan, his rare talents were quickly utilized by the pride of high society. To the upper classes, Waggenstef was a miracle worker: a last minute party could be thrown with his assistance and held in a banquet room, the event appearing to have been planned for days in advance. He could discretely acquire dinner reservations—when none had been made—with the blink of an eye.

And, unlike most maîtres, he never accepted a gratuity—never. He believed that it was his responsibility to serve. It was just that simple. He was paid to do his job, and if that required miracles, he would perform them as part of the day's work.

His duties at times were the same as a local bartender's in a neighborhood watering hole. Often his elite patrons would lower their guard to confess about a recent affair, a business venture gone wrong, or even, in one instance, a plan to take the life of a business rival.

Why would Manhattan's upper-crust confide in the unassuming man who stood only five-feet- five inches in height with a balding brow? The reason was simple: his premier talent was as valuable as a virtuoso violinist's—he had incredible technique but never showed off; he knew how to keep his mouth shut.

The popular hotel personality had a rather peculiar event take place on a Saturday night, one autumn evening, in nineteen-fifty-one.

Tyrone Power and guests arrived without a reservation to dine. In his inimitable way, Waggenstef managed to accommodate the film star on the spot. At the end of the evening Power was insistent that Willy accept a small gratuity for his performance above and beyond the call of duty.

That night changed Willard's life forever.

The star, finally exhausted from arguing for over thirty minutes about Willy's refusal to accept a tip, stood up and shouted so that all within range could hear. "…Well, Jesus Christ, Willy, if that's how you are then you should certainly come to Hollywood and offer your talents to my favorite hotel in Beverly Hills. There's not one honest son-of-a-bitch in the business south of Palm Springs!"

Both men laughed, but Tyrone Power was serious. It was a little known fact that the leading man had wisely invested his earnings in hotels in Hollywood: one of the first box-office draws to realize the fickleness of the industry.

Three weeks later, Waggenstef was onboard the Continental Pacific Flyer, rolling west at breakneck speed. Waiting for him when he arrived at Alameda station in downtown Los Angeles was a smiling Tyrone Power, besieged with fans and at the same time helping Willy with his luggage. Mr. Power's chauffer drove the two directly to the Beverly Hills Hotel on Sunset Boulevard. The hotel staff was assembled to greet them.

With the screen star's unforgettable smile and enthusiasm, he introduced the transplanted New Yorker to one and all and escorted him into the Polo Lounge, calling for champagne for everyone.

The short, amiable manager of the Polo Lounge at the Beverly Hills Hotel was one of Marilyn Monroe's favorite people in Hollywood. He had befriended the star a few years back when she was in need.

It was an impossible night, just days before the nineteen-fifty-nine Academy Awards presentation. A torrential storm dropped five inches of rain on the L.A. basin in less than four hours. *Some Like It Hot* was the hit of the year and up for several nominations. Marilyn had received the Golden Globe Award as best actress in a comedy or musical for her portrayal of a vagabond female musician in search of a man with money. It had been a challenging film due to rumors about her pregnancy. The cast had been wonderful to her, and especially the film's director, Billy Wilder. She had to laugh when she thought about all of the retakes that were necessary for the kissing scene with Tony Curtis. She was surprised by his nervousness. He was like a little boy who didn't know what to do.

Marilyn had booked into the Beverly Hills hotel a few days prior to the awards show to get away from the press. She busied herself pouring through some of her books and phonograph records she had sent over.

She was reading fragments from Plutarch's *Parallel Lives*, discovering the similarities of the ancients and modern man, while listening to Beethoven's late quartets—perfect for a rainy day. The hours passed by until she realized, around eight o'clock, that she was starving. The rain was pounding so fiercely on the roof that she was afraid to try and run across the property to the dining room.

She phoned room service.

They were very apologetic, but it was impossible for any of their staff to serve until the weather calmed down. They hoped she'd understand. The expanse of lawn between the hotel and her secluded suite was flooded. The hotel was not equipped to deliver room service in these severe weather conditions. Everything would be soaked by the time it arrived. They asked her to please be patient. They would contact her as soon as possible.

She said she understood. Naturally, her hunger increased as it seemed unlikely that she would be dining soon. She scoured through the two rooms to see if there was a left over Baby Ruth candy bar hiding in her purse or a packet of crackers in the desk drawer.

A few minutes later, there was a knock at her door. She had no appointments and wasn't expecting any friends. Panic set in. She was about to pick up the phone to inform the desk, when she heard a muffled voice through the pounding rain.

"Ms. Monroe, it is Willard Waggenstef, from the Polo Lounge. I have a meal for you."

Marilyn jumped to open the door. There, before her, stood the stout little man with arms fully extended holding a tray full of food and drink. He was soaking wet and brandishing his warm smile. The tray was miraculously dry.

Marilyn waved him inside. He took only one step across the threshold and set the tray down on the entry-way table.

"My apologies, Madame, I should have called you first to inform you that I was arriving, but there just wasn't time." A wry smile came over his face. "There are many like yourself who are also desperate for a meal."

Marilyn queried. "Well, why did you serve me before the others?"

The man bowed. "Because, madam, you were the only one who did not complain about the delay. I felt that your patience deserved a reward. I bid you bon appetite and good night."

With that, he turned around and disappeared under a sheet of rain.

The Darvon was within reach.

She would simply need to roll over to the other side of the bed. It was two a.m. She hadn't been able to sleep. One or two of the little pink pills usually offered the star a decent night's rest. She was awake because she was lonely.

"How odd," she thought, knowing that her fans who worshipped the image projected on the screen also thought her to be a whore, sleeping around every night with any man of her choice, for any reason, at any time.

She shook the bottle. She asked herself the age-old question: is it half-full, or half-empty? She tossed two pills into her mouth and swilled them down with a few sips of water. She stared at the bottle deciding it was half-full.

Scooping up the newspaper with the *Examiner's* review of Carl's poems, written by a young man she didn't know, she read it one more time. "This one *understands*," she thought.

Within minutes she could feel the Darvon taking effect: that familiar haziness as shifting clouds appeared to engulf her bed. The feeling of someone pushing her onto her back. The drug followed a predictable pattern. She fanned out her arms and legs picturing da Vinci's *Squaring the Circle* with the human body in the center. Her imagination set free—the same series of ancient images crept into place. She would have visions of Italy centuries ago. But tonight she could not place herself within the imaginary castle walls of medieval Europe.

She knew why she couldn't sleep: that *Life* magazine front page photo of her sitting at Carl's feet disturbed her. No one, including her press agent, had warned her that the image would be on the streets today. She was shocked when the magazine arrived before lunch. The photo for the cover was innocent, intimate, and introspective.

That was the problem.

People had no idea of who she really was, away from being a film star. This reality prompted the decision to take a bold step into her future.

Carl Sandburg filled a void in her life. She was never lonely knowing he was there for her. Their relationship was personal, away from Hollywood glitter and rumor. She decided, before falling asleep, that she must tell her story before someone else does it for her. The young journalist who wrote such an insightful review of Carl's poems might be the one to help her.

The lies and evil rumors, the tattle-tale columnists—all of these negatives which she lived with on a daily basis could be painful but were possible to deal with because, inside, she knew it was part of the game: the off-and-on personality she had created known as Marilyn Monroe.

She would meet with Rory Long to see if her feeling about him was correct.

His sensitivity towards Carl's verses, and the fact that he was young and new to Hollywood's circles of wheelers, dealers, and schemers, gave her confidence in her choice.

In her dazed condition she gazed at the cover photo again, feeling violated as if she had been raped by a stranger in a dark room.

There did not seem to be a way to protect those deep feelings that roamed around inside her: this fact was scarier than evil itself.

# Chapter 4

I arrived at the *Examiner* Tuesday Morning by nine o'clock sharp.

Word had spread about the call from Marilyn last night. I now had a clock on top of my otherwise barren desk, whose steady tick kept me checking the time.

*9:16 a.m.*

I typed her phone number and locked it in my desk drawer. Every once in while I checked my shirt pocket to make sure the key was still there.

I spread the Black Dahlia files on my desk, organized by date and category. One folder was a pile of black-and-white photos of the crime scene, and several varied publicity shots of the murdered would-be actress.

Elizabeth Short was very attractive but not as beautiful as Marilyn. One publicity photo in particular, of the girl reclining on a couch in a provocative pose, grabbed my attention. She was trying to look sexy. Marilyn never had to try. With her it was natural. She had charisma, personality, whatever you want to call it, which was not added on at a later date.

I jotted down a few notes as I culled through the hodgepodge of information. I was doing my best to stay focused, but pounding in the back of my skull was the phone call to *her* at ten o'clock.

*9:26 a.m.*

A middle-aged woman seated a few feet away left her desk and approached me with that type of smile that is a warning: this person wants something. My instinct was correct.

Bunny Blanchard, the *Women's Day* columnist, arrived with her hand extended spouting a barrage which began with "welcome to the staff... could you keep me informed of every word that passes between you and Miss Monroe... my readers would be so grateful if you would..." and so on.

When she finally came up for air, I attempted to introduce myself. "I'm Rory Long, nice to meet you." But the journalist was already on her way back to her desk giving me an enthusiastic wave. I'm sure she never heard me.

Was it my imagination, or was the clock ticking louder? I continued to sift through the various folders trying to stay calm.

Carol Thompson came over to tell me the boss wanted to talk before the call.

*9:46 a.m.*

I jumped from my desk and ran to Weisman's office. I knocked.

"It's open." Weisman was leaning back in his chair, hands folded across his chest with a huge grin on his face. "Well, well, if it isn't our local hero."

I looked beyond Weisman to the clock on his wall.

*9:52 a.m.*

I was beginning to sweat. I spoke timidly. "Sir, I've got that call at ten o'clock sharp and I don't want to miss…"

Weisman bolted up in his chair with a snap, startling me. "No, we don't want you to be late with this one." The editor lit a cigarette. "Just wanted to remind you that you are working for the *Examiner,* and as such, not a word of what Miss Monroe tells you goes beyond these walls until we decide what to print and what not to print," Weisman took a deep drag. "We on the same page, my young friend?"

I nodded while uttering a dry-throated, "Yes, sir!"

"Alright, go get'em, tiger." Weisman saluted and shooed me out of the office with both arms. I raced to my desk, took out the key, opened the drawer, and placed the phone in front of me. I didn't really need to look at the number; I'd memorized it last night before going to bed.

*9:59 a.m.*

I took a deep breath and picked up the receiver, eyes fixed on the second hand of the clock. How could it be moving so slowly? Ten o'clock struck. I dialed the number and waited.

All eyes were on me. One ring…two rings…three rings…four rings…I was going mad with anticipation.

Finally, someone picked up. "Miss Monroe's residence."

I hadn't counted on another person answering. "Good morning, this is Rory Long calling from the *Herald Examiner* for Miss Monroe…is she available?"

The voice said coldly, "Can you hold while I check?"

I thought I was going to throw up.

In what seemed an eternity, with no one on the other end of the line, I pressed the phone against my ear so hard that it gave me a headache.

Eventually, that unmistakable velvety voice drifted over the black Bakelite. "Rory, are you still there?"

I remembered what she'd said last night. I was to call her by her first name. "Yes, Marilyn, I'm here." A slight round of repressed laughter echoed through the newsroom. I looked up to find Weisman standing in the center of the room with his index finger to his lips signaling for silence.

Marilyn spoke first. "Well, I will have to give you an 'A' for punctuality, Rory. I admire a man who is on time."

I almost caved in. Talking to her now felt different than last night. Today, my mouth was not cooperating with my brain. "Well...I...thank you, Miss Monroe, I mean, Marilyn."

The film star laughed softly. "You seem nervous, Rory, but there is no reason to be."

"Yes, ma'am." Christ, I've done it again!

Monroe laughed louder. "My, my, you're aging me every time we speak!"

I looked up. The newsroom had come to a halt. Everyone was watching me. I composed myself, regained control, and shut the others out. "Marilyn, how can I be of service?"

For ten minutes I listened intently. All the voyeurs heard from my end were an occasional "Yes, Marilyn," or "I see...of course..." and finally "... that should be fine. Until then." I hung up.

I remained at my desk jotting down notes.

When I looked up, Weisman was in front of me. "Time for a coffee and a donut with the boss, kid. Grab your hat and coat and follow me."

I put her phone number back in my desk drawer and locked it. The moment had passed. Everyone on the floor was back plugging away at their assignments as the hammering of dozens of typewriters filled the room like a swarm of angry, metallic bees.

Weisman punched the button to call the elevator, his eyes scanning my exhausted figure.

"Well, kid, what did she have to say? She give you a dinner invitation or a date for lunch at Musso and Frank?"

The elevator arrived with a ding. I stepped into the unusually empty cabin. "She said that she didn't want to be remembered as a joke."

The elevator sped to the ground floor.

Weisman waited. "That's it? That's all she told you in ten minutes? You've got to be kidding me."

I was in a trance. "I need to eat. I'll explain it all after lunch."

"Okay, buddy, the pastrami's on me, then we chat."

I beamed. "I'd rather have a ham and cheese on rye."

The boss smiled back. "Whatever."

We rolled into Nat's Deli on eighth and Pico and grabbed a table. I took my last bite and pushed myself back from the empty dishes. The scraping noise grated like fingernails on a chalkboard.

Weisman was still at it but placed his sandwich back on his plate. "Okay, now that we have a full stomach, it's time to confess to the priest all of your sins. What did the lady have to say for herself, and what in the hell does she want from you?"

I belched, making an excuse with my arms extended, hands on the edge of the table for support. I was feeling weak as if I'd just run a race. "It's pretty simple actually." I looked around to see if anyone was listening: a paranoid gesture, normal to a newcomer in the business.

Weisman had a larger-than-life smile. "And…?"

"She wants me to meet her at the Polo Lounge next Sunday afternoon at three o'clock."

Weisman, gesturing with his hands, "And…?"

I chose my words. "She wants me, and only me, to tell her story: the story no one knows."

Weisman was beside himself.

A thousand different impulses shot through him like volts of electricity. What story? *Her secret love affairs? She's a heroin addict? She has a child hidden away in Bellflower?* The process wouldn't stop. "Okay, why you?" I shrugged my shoulders while finishing a crème soda. In those few moments of silence, Weisman was beginning to fit the pieces of the puzzle together.

"Oh, I get it. It's your review of Sandburg. She thinks you're an insightful journalist with that special, cultural sense of horseshit."

I responded with a look that told the editor that he'd stepped over the line.

Weisman backed off. "Alright, sweetheart, you're the greatest intellectual since Marshall McLuhan, but for God's sake and my blood pressure to boot, what the hell story does she feel that she can only share with a freshman newspaper journalist who hasn't even picked up his first paycheck?"

I offered a blank look. "That's a secret between Marilyn and myself. It's a condition she made when she proposed this one-on-one interview for as long as it takes next Sunday. She made me promise not to tell anyone, particularly you…"

Weisman straightened his back resembling a prairie dog looking out of his hole. "She mentioned my name?"

I smiled. "I wouldn't be too gleeful. She told me not to trust you. Evidently there was an article in the *Herald* last year: a rumor about her and another Hollywood star who was in the middle of divorcing his second wife. The article you printed showed up in the weekend edition as if it were gospel. She told me you had assured her that all of the sources would be confirmed before the article went to print. She said they weren't."

He quickly recalled the incident. He also recalled firing the reporter. "Well, kid, you can't win 'em all. I cut the journalist from the payroll and tore Hedda Hopper a new asshole over that event. It was the failed actress turned gossip columnist who started the rumor in the first place."

I mimicked my boss. "Whatever."

He smiled.

I gathered up my hat and coat. "Anyway, that's where it's at. She has taken me into her confidence, and for all that's worth, I'm sticking to her request."

We locked eyes.

Weisman folded. He knew the game better than most. Okay, the youngster has ethics. It won't take him long to lose sight of those principles: there's no room for such things in this business. For now, there really isn't any problem.

Rory will interview the star, then type out his notes in triplicate at his desk. The *Examiner* owns the information as long as the kid is employed by the company. And oh, he will be, at least until this story is concluded.

Weisman relaxed the tension in his facial muscles and called for the check. "This one's on me, pal. You'd better get back to the newsroom and dive into the Dahlia files. I still want that article the day before you meet Miss *I've Got a Secret* Sunday afternoon."

As Rory headed back to the office, the savvy editor ordered an extra dry martini, sitting alone for a few minutes and sipping it slowly while taking a tally of points he might score when this interview hits the stands.

# Chapter 5

I'd never been to the Polo Lounge at the Beverly Hills Hotel on Sunset. I'd only seen pictures in magazines. The cozy, dark wood-paneled atmosphere seemed like a movie set. It was a long way from where I was now, at my desk downtown.

I will meet Marilyn Monroe at this famous bar in five days to interview her at her request. She had a story. On the phone with her this morning, she said; "I need to do this. You're just beginning your career. I'm taking a chance on you."

It was time to talk to mom in Boulder. What would grandfather have thought? I was born three years after the Louisiana politician was assassinated by his opponents.

*"Every man a king."*

I was fascinated with Huey Long from the time I could read. I devoured his books and the dozens of articles penned in his lifetime. I think I became a journalist because of my mother and grandfather.

Was he a radical?

The man believed the wealthy should share their bounty with the poor. Huey Long was for assisting the masses who had not been as fortunate as others to get them back on their feet.

F. D.R. labeled him, "…one of the most dangerous men in America." To me, he was simply a visionary with a big heart. I kept my heritage and blood-line a secret. I didn't want people to be influenced, in any direction, because I was a direct descendent of Huey Long.

His only daughter, Rose, gave birth to me when she was still a teenager. She had been grandmother's secretary when nana took over her husband's senate seat after he was buried. But she had me to raise, so Rose cut her ties to politics and concentrated on my upbringing. She encouraged me to think independently, to follow my passion. At the same time, as a member of the Long family, she feared for my future. If I happened to pursue a career in politics, she felt I would be pressured by my background.

Six o'clock rolled around without a surprise phone call from a Hollywood star. I headed for the bus stop. I needed to hear my mother's voice. The anticipation of a Sunday afternoon spent in a darkly lit room in Beverly Hills, conversing with the most beautiful and well-known woman on the planet, was something I couldn't wait to share with her.

As the bus trudged its way slowly through rush-hour traffic, all seemed peaceful and calm except what was going through my mind.

When I got home, I raced to the phone.

I called and let it ring a dozen times, but there was no answer. I lit a cigarette to calm myself down. Suddenly, all of the events in the past forty-eight hours took their toll. I began to have doubts. Was I really up to the task of spending an afternoon talking intimately with the Hollywood star? Wouldn't she realize, within minutes, that she had made a mistake?

The phone rang.

I grabbed it. "...Hello?"

The voice responded with a slight chuckle. "Rory, it's Rose. Was it you who called a few minutes ago?" Mother's instinct.

Ever since I was a teenager, I'd called my mother by her Christian name. She was more than a mom. She was a friend and confidant.

She listened attentively as I explained what had taken place in the past two days. When I finished, there was silence.

"Rose, you still there?"

"Well, this is a bit much for me to take in all at once. Of course I'm very proud of you and this could be your big break. Everything seems to be happening so fast."

I sensed hesitation. "What's the matter? Do you think I've made a mistake? Am I in over my head?"

Huey Long's only daughter was very used to public opinion. It had dogged her all of her life. But she was also a mother who knew her son came from a bloodline ready to do battle if that became the case. She quickly turned her mood around. "You're a Long, Rory, you can handle it."

Her voice became joyful. "Okay, tell me what you're going to wear. Do you have a good suit? I mean, if you're going to be seen in public with Marilyn Monroe, you need to be dressed correctly. Will I get a picture of the two of you together that I can show off to my bridge club?"

I laughed like a valve opening to relieve the tension.

"Well, hells-bells, my son has a date with a movie star. How many mothers in America can boast about that tonight?"

After we hung up, I grabbed a beer and a sandwich from the kitchen and sat down with the Black Dahlia, ready to dig in.

# Chapter 6

Weisman was in his office waiting for Rory. With no real purpose, he shuffled stacks of papers on his desk under the pretense he was organizing.

Normally, Saturday mornings were reserved for eighteen holes at Roosevelt, in Griffith Park, with rival editor Syd Gould from the *Tribune*. His friend was a lousy golfer who claimed to have a six handicap. For years, Allan had known Syd's real handicap was the fact that he had absolutely no talent for the game. Gould swiped at the ball as if he were swatting a pesky fly. Weisman used the pocket money he picked up every weekend to pay for his lunches during the week. But today was different.

It was a few minutes before ten. The cub reporter was due any minute; the kid would be dropping off his article. If Rory came up with a new angle on the Dahlia that might grab their readers, then Allan could give the kid a run on the paper for the long haul. Of course, the other reason for meeting up with the newest member on his staff was to have a pep talk about his interview with Marilyn Monroe scheduled for tomorrow.

Somehow, Rory led a charmed life.

One day on the job and he caught the attention of the most elusive star in Hollywood. It must run in the family. Weisman was mesmerized by a dust cloud floating around in the morning sunrays, which poured through high windows of the office.

In a trance, he was reviewing the surprise that was waiting for him when he returned home last night.

When the Editor-in-Chief pulled up to his house, he found a dark sedan parked in the driveway. After his persecution, spearheaded by Joe McCarthy in the early fifties, he could smell law enforcement and government agents a mile away. He parked on the street and bounced through the front door as he always did.

"Margaret, I'm home. Where are you darling?"

His wife of twenty-eight years knew, by the way he called out, that he was aware of the situation. "Oh, I'm in here, dear. We have visitors."

Weisman burst into the living room. He pretended to not notice the two men dressed in dark suits and still wearing their hats in the presence of a lady. They must be Federal Agents.

He gave his wife a kiss on the cheek and turned around swiftly, "Gentlemen, please tell me what has brought two representatives of the United States Government to my home this gorgeous Friday evening?"

The two men looked at each other.

Allan poured himself a scotch. He didn't offer them one. Weisman had been through hell during the McCarthy era. He was called upon by the Senator's committee to give testimony against his colleagues, some of the most talented journalists and writers in the business.

His associates were suspected of being Communists. Weisman refused to cooperate and was handed down a thirty-day jail sentence. He took it in stride, writing about the experience while incarcerated, which garnered a *Peabody* after the article was published in the *New Yorker*. Although this event took place eight years ago, Weisman knew his name was still in J. Edgar Hoover's little black book.

The heavier-set agent spoke first. "We are of the understanding that you have a new employee at your paper, one…" Weisman noted the dramatic pause used to intimidate. He knew the son-of-a-bitch didn't have to consult his note book for the name. "…Rory Daniel Long. Is that correct?"

Weisman was trying to figure out where this was going. The kid was too shy to be a subversive. "Yeah, Mr. Long started his first week with us Monday. Is there a problem?"

The second agent, a tall, gaunt figure took over. "Were you aware, Mr. Weisman, that Mr. Long is the son of Rose Long McClellan, the daughter of Huey Long?"

"Jesus," Weisman thought to himself, "Are these guys desperate for something to do, or what?"

He downed his scotch. "Actually, I had no idea that the kid was related to Huey Long. Again, is there a problem?"

The first agent answered. "Well, as far as we know, not at the moment. We were just asked to stop by to make you aware of the fact. We'd like you to keep an eye on him, make sure he doesn't get out of control."

Weisman was way pissed-off, but he knew better than to cause a ruckus in his own home. He set down his empty glass and approached the men with his arms held out, indicating that it was time for them to leave. "Well, I'll certainly warn all of our female staff that he might be on the prowl," Weisman paused to wink, "…but if you took a gander at the women on our staff, you'd feel very comfortable about Rory Long's capacity to behave himself."

The thin man spoke as Weisman escorted them to his front door. "You know what we mean, Mr. Weisman. I'm sure that you will carefully edit whatever Long submits for publication."

He threw open his front door. "Oh, I can assure you I will take charge of every single word that comes off of his typewriter. Good evening, gentlemen, have a nice dinner." With that, Weisman slammed the door shut. He heard them walking away, and in a few seconds, they started their car and pulled out.

He returned to the living room, where Margaret remained seated. "Another scotch, sweetheart?"

Weisman gave Margaret a tense smile. "Just give me the damn bottle."

# Chapter 7

## My brain ached from research.

The Black Dahlia case led to a dead end in the primary investigation. After reviewing the accumulated testimony, newspaper articles, and police reports, I'd come up with one possible scenario.

A detective named Malcolm Stoddard from the Hollywood precinct was assigned to the case, then reassigned the following day. I had a copy of his notes. The penmanship was crude. He wrote like a grammar school student. It was that, or the man was very nervous during his brief inquiry. I also found something odd penciled on the margin of one page of his report: a doodle of an emblem used by the medical profession—a snake wrapped around a cross.

I did a background check. His father was a doctor. The body of Elizabeth Short had been cut in two and all of the blood drained off. It seemed logical that this type of heinous crime could only be perpetrated by someone in the medical field. Someone with the knowledge and experience it would take to cut a body in two: a doctor who was also a surgeon.

Was the detective worried that his father may have done this, or that someone in his father's circle may have been responsible? Why was he taken off this case?

It was getting late. I still had to type up my report and hand it over to the boss at ten o'clock in the morning. I rolled the first page of blank paper into my Remington; the clatter of keys, along with the bell-ring at the end of each line, kept me awake until midnight, when I finally finished.

At nine-thirty Saturday morning, I gulped down my coffee at Woolworth's while proofreading the article one more time. I exited the elevator at the sixth floor and walked toward Weisman's office. It was an eerie feeling. The weekend crew was hard at it finalizing the Sunday edition. The newsroom was nearly empty. Through the stilled atmosphere, I could make out Weisman's figure moving around behind frosted windows.

"Right on time, good man." He offered me a chair. At least this time I wouldn't have to stand at attention. I handed him my article. He read silently, taking his time as I fidgeted. When he finished, he carefully aligned the sheets and placed them in the center of his desk. He leaned back in his chair. "So, you think that one of our city's illustrious medical practitioners was responsible for this crime? And you also believe that the *Herald Examiner* could take a chance and print your opinion, knowing that some crackpot attorney who represents the medical council of Los Angeles County might take the paper to court?"

I was about to throw up my breakfast. I started to defend myself. "Look, I worked all week on this…"

Weisman jumped in. "I don't care if you spent the past year reassessing the Black Dahlia murder: facts are facts."

I waited for the knockout punch.

He surprised me with a smile. "To tell you the truth, I felt the same way when the case first broke. It seemed to me that it would be impossible for John Q. Public to pull this off." He lit a cigarette. "We'll run it in Monday's evening edition. That will give us a tranquil night before the fireworks." Weisman offered me a cigarette. I accepted it eagerly. "Well done, young man." Weisman's eyes burned into mine. "But I would expect nothing less than excellence from Huey Long's grandson."

I choked on the smoke. He laughed. "Take it easy, kid. I just found out about your family last night." His mood changed. "Two of our Government's finest were waiting for me when I got home."

I opened my mouth.

Weisman waved me off. "I just wanted you to know that the Feds are aware you're on the payroll." Weisman's big smile returned. "To tell you the truth, kid, I can't wait to publish your interview with Marilyn. That bastard J. Edgar Hoover has been all over her case. He thinks she's sleeping with the Kennedys!"

I stubbed out my cigarette. "Well, I hope you understand why I didn't tell you. I've always thought that it could work against me, as well as for me. I just want to stand on my own two feet."

The veteran newsman became all business. "Frankly, son, I don't give a shit from whose womb you popped out. But, by the way, you've handled yourself in your first week on the job; there is a slight chance of a future for you in this business. Huey Long's grandson or not, you've got printer's ink in your blood." Weisman reached for his coat. "Jesus, I'll have to thank Syd for recommending you to the paper as I whip the pants off him next Saturday."

I was about to ask for advice about my interview with Monroe, when he beat me to the punch.

"As far as tomorrow goes, keep these two things in mind: she called you; you're there at her invitation." Weisman stood to leave. "Also, your only responsibility is to report, as accurately as possible, what she says and how she feels."

Weisman crushed his cigarette into the ashtray with force as he glanced at my Dahlia article centered on his desk. "Get a good night's sleep. I'll see you bright and early Monday morning."

# Chapter 8

*Sleep* was like a word from a foreign language. My body had no idea what it meant as I tossed and turned in anticipation of my interview with Marilyn.

What the hell did I expect? I was no stranger to insomnia. It led me to this day.

When the sun seeped through the crack in the curtain, I gave up. I stood barefoot in my wrinkled pajamas, staring at the coffee pot and begging it to percolate.

After two cups, I packed my briefcase with notepads, pencils, and pens. As a second thought, I included Kleenex and a small flashlight; the interior of most bars was dark.

By eight a.m., I'd finished breakfast and returned to bed, dragging along the briefcase.

During the week, I'd jotted down a list of potential questions. In a daze from lack of sleep and the caffeine pumping up my heart rate, I realized this list was useless.

I didn't have the slightest idea what she wanted to talk about except that she had asked me to avoid questions about her film career or show business in general. All week long, one thing she'd said kept echoing inside my brain: *I don't want to be remembered as a joke.*

I woke up in a panic at one o'clock. I'd fallen asleep. I bolted, and my briefcase, with all its contents, flew around the room. I scurried to pick things up like a squirrel gathering nuts, then jumped into the shower and experienced a minor panic attack. My breathing became narrow and rapid, but streams of steaming water calmed me down.

At a quarter past two, the cab arrived. I was not going to chance waiting for a bus. The driver pulled up to the Beverly Hills Hotel at two-forty-five. Walking toward the lobby, I spied the entrance to the Polo Lounge. I stepped inside, pausing to adjust my eyes to the dark.

A short, bald man in a tuxedo approached me. He spoke with a foreign accent. "Allow me to introduce myself. I am Willard Waggenstef, the concierge of the hotel and manager of the Polo Lounge." His mustache arched upward as he moved close to me and whispered, "By chance, would you happen to be the young man scheduled for an interview with one of our regular clients at three o'clock?"

I nodded.

He made a slight bow and I followed him to a leather-tufted booth in the back of the room. There was a Chinese-silk dressing screen covering the width for privacy. I slid in. The concierge asked me if I'd like a drink. I really wanted a dry-as-dust martini, but I asked for a coke.

He smiled.

Marilyn was late.

I took out my notebook and three pencils. I was wondering what I planned to do with them. My anxiety grew by the second. I tried to distract myself by glancing around the room.

Oil paintings of horses riding crops and rows of trophies under glass adorned the walls: artifacts of the game, the winners, and losers. Scattered about the bar were a multitude of framed, black-and-white photos of prominent film stars and their steeds, polo mallet in hand at the ready. This place appeared more like a museum that served cocktails than a bar.

A figure rushed through the entrance, greeted eagerly by the concierge, and the pair headed my way. I didn't recognize her. She wore a black wig and a floppy hat along with huge sunglasses and a frumpy, oversized coat. Marilyn slid into the opposite side of the booth. Waggenstef pulled the Chinese screen into place. I was in shock. She removed her disguise and held out her hand.

"It's a pleasure to meet you, Rory."

I shook her hand gently. Just to touch Marilyn was electric. I couldn't believe this was happening. "It's my pleasure, Ms. Monroe."

She waved her free index finger at me. "It's Marilyn, don't forget that." We laughed.

Waggenstef arrived with a Manhattan and another coke. She held her glass up to propose a toast. "To a very pleasant afternoon."

My smile hurt my face.

Marilyn took a deep breath. "You ready?"

I took up a pencil and opened my notebook. The hour had finally arrived.

The most recognizable woman on the planet started things off by asking me a question. I thought that was my job.

"Tell me, Rory, do you like music…I mean, real music?" Marilyn fidgeted with her cocktail glass and seemed uncharacteristically shy.

The question threw me. "I suppose so…but what do you mean by *real* music?"

Marilyn let out one of her patented giggles. "Well, you see, when I first came to Hollywood, I was being hustled by men attached to the studios." She paused to take a sip. "One time, a famous director asked me out for dinner and I turned him down because he didn't know who Béla Bartók was: he'd never heard his string quartets. It seemed reasonable to me at the time. I mean, why should I want to date a man who had never listened to Bartók? Does that make sense to you?"

I was stunned. Jesus Christ, I'm in my mid-twenties and haven't been around the world yet. I wasn't sure what was going on, but my instinct told me that this might be a test of some kind to see if I can keep up. Frankly, I wasn't sure that I could, but fortunately in this case, luck was with me.

My former girlfriend at UCLA was the second violinist in the campus string quartet and I had actually heard all of Bartók's quartets in one season on campus. I didn't remember much about them except that the first one seemed prettier than the others.

"Well, I like the first one the best. It was easier to listen to. I didn't hear much melody in the others."

Marilyn nodded in approval. She seemed to have forgotten her question. "Yes, Rory, I felt the same way when I first listened to his music. But sometimes, things that are serious, well thought-out, and reaching for places beyond what we are used to understanding take time to appreciate."

Philosophy, not diamonds, appeared to be this girl's best friend. I jotted down her thought.

"So, what did the director say when you turned him down?"

Marilyn laughed. "He told me I didn't stand a chance of making it in motion pictures!"

I had to pinch myself. There I was, sitting in the Polo Lounge in Beverly Hills with Marilyn Monroe, cracking jokes. I was sure I'd wake up soon.

Monroe wasn't finished with Bartók. "I heard a great story about the Hungarian genius from Yehudi Menuhin." She became excited as if she were about to divulge a closely guarded secret.

"It was Menuhin who commissioned one of the solo violin or viola concertos from Bartók. He felt sorry for the man when he found out that he was nearly impoverished. So, Menuhin contacted Bartók, who was living in New York at the time. They agreed upon an advance price of two thousand dollars. The composer didn't want to take the money, but the violinist insisted."

There was a light tap on the Chinese screen. Marilyn looked at me with that you-check-it-out expression. I poked my head around. It was Waggenstef, refreshing our drinks along with two menus from the dining room.

She continued. "So, the day comes when Menuhin arrives back in New York to play the concerto for the composer. Yehudi is shocked to find Bartók living at the YMCA. The composer is in a small room, dressed in a suit, sitting at a table with a copy of the music and a pencil and eraser—just like the professor that he was most of his life. Menuhin is bemused. He plays the piece in its entirety. When the last note fades, Bartók stands with tears in his eyes, telling the violinist that he never thought he'd hear the piece played so beautifully and accurately in his lifetime."

Marilyn traced her finger around the lip of her glass. She giggled at her own story. "And the follow up was even more revealing." Her blonde curls touched the top of the table as she leaned toward me in a whispery voice. "As broke as Bartók was, he hadn't cashed Menuhin's check yet because he wasn't sure that the violinist would like his composition."

Her cleavage distracted me as I grinned, trying to hide my reaction. At one moment, her right nipple became exposed, and I almost fainted. What had I gotten myself into? Fear and anxiety were about to mix their own cocktail of pure panic.

I couldn't justify the reason for my being with her even though, as Weisman pointed out, she made the choice. Still, I felt completely out of place. I barely knew who Bartók was. Who's next? How in the hell will I be able to keep up? I came out of this all-consuming trance to find her staring at me.

"Hey, you okay?"

I stumbled around for an answer as if I were trying to find the light switch in an unfamiliar room. "Yeah, I'm fine…I mean, I was just thinking about something and, uh, I…"

The actress was halfway through her second Manhattan, and the sun was still up. She reached across the table and took my hand. "Don't worry, they won't shoot the messenger." She gave my hand a squeeze. "I want to tell my story. I'm just beginning to understand it myself, so, you see, I'm just as unsure as you are. We're a perfect match."

Willy came to take our orders. Marilyn didn't look at the menu; she knew it by heart. She ordered oysters on the half-shell and a salad. My mind was going a million miles a minute. I couldn't concentrate enough to decide what to order. The Swiss concierge smiled, telling me not to worry; he'd bring me something that would hold me for the afternoon.

A faraway look came over her and she began to talk about Arthur Miller. "You know, Rory, Arthur was a very shy man, and the first one to put me in touch with myself."

I was caught off-guard with this subject. "What do you mean? Didn't you know who you were before you met him?"

She stared down at her drink as she spoke. 'Well, I thought I did, but, Rory, I've never been very sure of myself. Arthur encouraged my intellectual side. He gave me confidence in my own style of self-education. We spent long evenings drinking and talking about literature and philosophy. Arthur never made me feel inferior. Quite the opposite, he admired my brain, and that was a lot more than most men had taken notice of."

She changed gears. "However, late-night discussions with Truman Capote were mostly laugh-riots. He is one of the funniest men I've ever met. His wit is nonstop. Some afternoons, while I was living in New York, we would meet at a café in the village and he would entertain me for hours with improvised comments on people passing by."

Talking Kierkegaard with Arthur Miller and Truman Capote, the circus clown.

I was beginning to see the process by which this woman wove her way through this obstacle course known as life. One of the most desirable creatures in the world was curious: she needed to know, and as insecure as her professional personality may have been, her intellect showed no fear.

Her brief reflection on Arthur Miller launched Marilyn into talking about her library of nearly four hundred books. She became animated. I was astounded that she could name most of them.

The collection included current literary masterpieces by Steinbeck, Hemingway, James Joyce, O'Neil, Dostoevsky, Proust, Victor Hugo, Dorothy Parker, along with the poets and playwrights: Dylan Thomas, Ezra Pound, John Montague, W. B. Yeats, Oscar Wilde, Poe, Emerson, Thoreau, and Emily Dickenson as well as Shakespeare, Sydney, Donne, Dante, and Petrarch. Then there were her books on theatre, acting, and the history of her profession. Marilyn considered herself an actress, not a film star.

While listing some of her library of books on theatre, she began to talk about Lee Strasberg, and she couldn't stop.

I could hear more voices in the bar. It was nearly five-thirty. The early crowd of would-be actors, agents, and screenwriters were gathering, full of forced laughter, hoping to rub elbows with the real actors, agents, and screenwriters.

"Lee saved my life." Marilyn tossed down the rest of her second drink. "That's the truth. I was so unsure of myself when I first went to New York to join the Actor's Studio, that after the first few sessions I thought about killing myself." She paused and gave me a flash of a smile that vanished abruptly. "Then, at one of our classes, he said something that changed my life."

The alcohol was taking effect. Marilyn was wandering away from the playing field. My nerves were frayed from trying to keep up with her. "What did Mr. Strasberg say?"

Marilyn let out a roar that came close to a scream. I was sure those in the bar would be tearing down the curtain any moment now. She collected herself. "Sorry, but you see, I've never heard anyone refer to Lee as *Mr.* Strasberg. He has always been Lee to everyone around him." Marilyn looked up hoping to find Willy there with another drink.

"One day, Lee made a simple statement; I mean, so simple that I should have thought of it myself. He merely said that the difference between an actor and a suicide victim was confidence. Just that simple: confidence." She looked at me wide-eyed with that what-can-I-tell-you expression.

"You mean that when Mr. Strasberg, I mean, Lee, said that… you decided not to kill yourself?"

"Well, it took some time. But when I told him that I was depressed while filming, he told me that Chaplin, Garbo, and Bergman were also depressed when they worked. He gave me a hug and said I was in good company!"

Suddenly, she sat up straight. Her body became rigid. She sobered up in a matter of seconds. "Well, Rory, we're getting away from our subject. I said there was to be no discussion about show business or acting."

The change in Monroe's personality disturbed me. I felt that a stranger had just slipped into our booth. I rolled with it. "Right. Shall we get back to your library?"

The blonde bombshell snapped back into the game. She searched through her oversized handbag and withdrew a journal. She scooted around the horseshoe-shaped booth to be next to me so we could both read from it. My thoughts at the moment with her hip touching mine could not be printed in my article for the *Examiner*.

With much enthusiasm, she traced her text with her index finger, explaining each section to its conclusion. Her nail polish was a bright, fire-engine red. Her cheek was close to mine. Her perfume was intoxicating. I felt a bulge in my pants. I downed my second Coca-Cola and it went away. I wasn't sure how much time had elapsed since she arrived. Every second went by like a minute, and for some reason, I didn't look at my watch.

I wanted this to go on forever.

As I watched Marilyn sifting through her journal, I was struck by the fact that her public persona had disappeared, replaced by a contented woman searching through her private thoughts and surprised by what she found.

She spent the next twenty minutes discussing her thoughts on Homer, Virgil, and Ovid's *Metamorphosis*. The more I sat in a dark corner booth of a bar in Beverly Hills, listening to professor Monroe explain the philosophy of ancient poets, the more incredible the day became.

I nibbled away at a tray full of raw vegetables, crackers, and cheese as she launched into a lecture on the history of modern civilization that could have been delivered to a Harvard humanities class.

What's next?

I'd taken down as much information as possible, but I felt I'd traveled up a blind alley, not sure if there was a way out. Who in the world will buy the fact that Hollywood's top sex symbol has an intellect that's off the charts? What was Weisman going to think? How in the hell was the world going to react? Christ, I thought to myself, she should be spending this time with Einstein, not a freshman journalist who hasn't been on the job more than a week.

Time was slipping by. I could hear more voices at the bar. Marilyn put her black wig and sunglasses on. I thought she was getting ready to leave. She excused herself to go the ladies room. She took the booth phone and punched two buttons. Waggenstef arrived shortly to escort her.

I felt very alone.

This was not my world. I was sweating heavily from stress and tension. I felt perspiration on my brow, under my arms, and along my spine. I tried to estimate how much longer I'd have with her.

Had she already said what she wanted to say, or was she just beginning? Did she have a clue about where she wanted to go with this interview? Was all of this about just not being remembered as a *joke?"*

Marilyn returned, refreshed. She took out another journal and scanned the pages searching through her poems. "When I listen to records, like the late quartets of Beethoven, or Respighi or Ravel's sonata for violin, poetry just gushes out of me." She ruffled her hair: "It's really automatic. The minute the needle stops scratching and I hear the first strains, I write."

Her red lips, encircling the whitest teeth I'd ever witnessed; her arms raised, fingers running through her blonde locks—I considered this moment to be the closest thing to sex anyone could experience without actually having it. She couldn't even turn her head without arousing a sexual emotion in whoever was near her at the time.

Marilyn sifted through her poems as if she were reading them for the first time. Her lips moved in silent concentration... those lips. My God, even the mere act of mouthing words was sensual. She flipped a page. A folded piece of paper fell onto the table. She read it while biting her lower lip.

"This is a poem that Carl wrote for me just before I left."

I couldn't resist looking over her shoulder at the document. It was typed on his personal stationary. The heading read, *Carl Sandburg, Poet*. The title was, *Marilyn*. It was a short poem of thirteen lines. She read it to me.

*Marilyn*
*I built a castle beneath the sea,*
*Just for you and me.*
*With my hands I stacked*
*Rock on top of rock,*
*On top of rock, on top, on top.*

*And in the morning,*
*All will be gone,*
*Like the plaintive melody*
*Of an unknown song,*
*Never sung,*
*Unheard by anyone.*

*I built a castle beneath the sea,*
*Just for you and me.*

The poem was child-like. It was juvenile in some way while still sounding as if it were coming from a well-traveled mind. When Marilyn finished reading, she sat frozen, staring at the poem.

She nodded her head up and down while slowly tapping the page with her index finger. "You know what, Rory?" She cleared her throat. "I've loved this man since the moment we met, three years ago. I mean, I fell in love with him the minute we were introduced." She sighed, letting all of the air out of her lungs. "And, of course, he is old enough to be my father, maybe even my grandfather."

I watched her profile. A tear had formed in the corner of her right eye.

"I never understood this verse because it was not the language of powerful images contained in most of his work." She folded the paper and put it in her purse. "I've read that poem over and over, and now, just now, at this moment, I understand it. Isn't that something?"

Waggenstef arrived with a third Manhattan. He must be telepathic. She took a slow sip while thinking things through.

Marilyn began to explain the poem as her forefinger traced the rim of the glass. "He's telling me that he loves me, but that our age difference and commitments to others prevent us from ever being together. The love he shares with me is a place: the castle he built, and it will be gone with the new day. What we have between us is like an unknown song which can never be sung—never be shared."

She sat upright with an all-knowing smile, like someone who had just come out of a dark tunnel.

"He knows that our feelings will be dispersed, like rocks stacked under the sea when the waves topple them, leaving no trace of their existence."

I stopped breathing when she finished.

I don't mean I held my breath; I literally stopped breathing. Somehow, I had witnessed a crucial moment in her life. The more time I spent with the film star, the more I was convinced that she must be the loneliest person on the planet. I wanted to hold her in my arms just to offer her comfort.

It was nearly seven o'clock.

We'd been at it for nearly three and a half hours. The bar sounded full. I was sure the Chinese screen would soon be trashed any minute now. Someone with a few shooters in them might answer the call of curiosity. I was relying on the concierge to prevent that, but I felt my time with her was limited nevertheless.

Marilyn returned to her poetry. I watched her. She seemed to be perfectly at peace. A glow came over her. I believed that examining her thoughts gathered between these pages had initiated a search for the intangible self. At this moment, nothing about Hollywood was reflected in her eyes.

When she looked up, I was smiling at her smile. She reacted as if I'd caught her with her hand in the cookie jar. "What is it, Rory?"

I felt trapped. "Oh, nothing…I was just looking at you, lost in your thoughts, and for a brief moment, you weren't Marilyn Monroe."

Supporting her head with one hand, her arm on the table, she leaned toward me with that glazed look of intoxicating contentment that was occasionally caught by the camera in rare moments of her films. "So, who was I, Rory? Tell me about the part of me that isn't Marilyn Monroe."

Something inside took over. Being around her was cathartic. I knew I was speaking, for I recognized my voice; I knew that the words were mine, but my perception at the moment was on another level, as if I were outside of the picture looking in—an impartial observer who had stopped by to evaluate.

"I see a woman with an intelligence that knows no bounds, who, left on her own, would happily toss her public life into the nearest ditch and escape to a peaceful solitude, where she would spend her remaining years fulfilling her wildest dreams: discovering the past and imagining her place in it."

The words spilled out of my mouth before I had a chance to screen them. When I finished, Marilyn looked as if she'd seen a ghost. Total paranoia came over me. My intuition told me that I had crossed a border in her map of the self, which was off limits to strangers.

"Rory, you astound me. That is exactly what I have been thinking about for years."

Just as quickly as she confirmed her innermost desire, she did an about-face and returned to her position in the universe. She transformed into Marilyn Monroe so quickly it shocked me.

"Rory, this has been great fun, but I have to go now. I will call you for another interview in a few days."

Marilyn was slurring her speech. Three Manhattans seemed to have run their course. She was giving me the heave-ho.

Did I get too close for comfort?

I could have shot myself. My nerves were on edge as she gathered up her belongings in haste and threw on her disguise. She exited the booth before I could even say goodbye. The bar was jammed with drinkers and hustlers. The minute Marilyn was gone, Waggensteff removed the screen. He gave me a wink. "I'm afraid I will need this booth. May I offer you a choice seat at our bar?"

I flashed a brief smile and waved him off, asking for the bill. He bowed slightly and told me madam had taken care of it. My energy was depleted. Everything was in slow motion. Nothing I brought with me fit back in my briefcase.

I was struggling to get the lid closed when I spied a notebook wedged into the crevasse of the leather booth. I scooped it up and put it in my jacket pocket.

As I walked out of the Polo Lounge after a Sunday afternoon in the company of the most famous woman in the world, I wasn't sure what hit me.

# Chapter 9

Allan Weisman was a man driven by the desire to report, as accurately as possible, the news of the day to his readers. He was younger than Rory when he started, and like all career persons with aspiring goals, he soon learned that playing the game wasn't always easy. To search for a glimpse of light, farther down the tunnel, may demand bending the rules, especially if the need to protect the rights of others arises.

Early on, he found a hobby that allowed him to put aside the pressures of his job for a few hours a week. He discovered the world of collecting postal stamps: he became a dedicated philatelist.

Margaret was relieved when her husband became a fanatic. It was the only time she knew him to be at peace.

In his den, on a quiet Sunday afternoon, the same day his newest employee was interviewing Marilyn Monroe, he picked up his latest find with a pair of tweezers and began to examine it with a magnifying glass.

His eyes focused on the enlarged image, slowly scanning the surface: an un-canceled, two-cent stamp issued by the U.S. Postal service in nineteen-twenty, honoring the Wright Brother's flight at Kitty Hawk. It was worth a small fortune. He found the item while browsing through a thrift shop on Fairfax Boulevard. It was on a post card that was never mailed. He paid a dollar for it. He should've been jubilant. This stamp was the best find since he began collecting. But no party hats today.

His mind was still sifting through Friday night's visit from two of J. Edgar's merry men. He could easily spot a warning shot across the bow.

He eased back in his chair and lit a cigarette.

His red telephone rang. This wasn't the household line. It was a private number that very few people had: a few friends and rivals. It shocked him. He sat up quickly. The fragile stamp floated to the floor.

Weisman picked up after one ring. "…Hello?"

Nothing.

All he could hear was an echo, as if he were in a tunnel. This hollow sound meant the caller could be long distance. He waited for a few seconds and was about to hang up when a woman spoke.

"Mr. Weisman, I have Mr. Hoover on the line for you. Are you clear to take his call?"

*Speak of the Devil!*

The senior editor was in a quandary. Hoover had sent his thugs over for a visit, and now he wanted to follow up.

"Yes, I am clear."

That unmistakable voice began. "Mr. Weisman, I felt that you and I should have a little chat about current affairs."

The editor shot back. "That's fine."

Allan could hear papers being shuffled. "I'm told that you have Huey Long's grandson in your employ."

"Correct."

Allan decided to move things along. "Is there something I should know?" He already thought he knew where this was going. The Bureau must have found out about the interview with Monroe. Hoover has been all over her case. "Your two representatives requested that I keep an eye on Long." Weisman really wanted to say *fuck you.* "Anything else?"

Hoover sighed. "Yeah, take Mr. Long off the Dahlia story. We are re-opening the case, and publicity at this point can't help."

Silence.

"Do we have an understanding Mr. Weisman?"

"Yes." It would be a piece-of-cake for the Bureau to find out about the Monroe interview, but how in the hell could Hoover know about Rory's Black Dahlia assignment? Only three people knew about it: Rory, Carol, and himself. Weisman wasn't expecting the freshman journalist to solve the riddle; he was just busting the kid's ass to break him in.

Is there an informant in the newsroom, passing information along to Hoover and his pals? On top of it, Hoover sounded anxious. Is one of the most powerful figures in American law enforcement being pressured to reinvestigate the Dahlia case, or the opposite? Is he trying to shut down any further investigations for the sake of protecting someone, or some group, who may have recently been connected to the brutal murder?

Weisman's head was about to explode. He pushed the envelope. "First Amendment aside, the article is on my desk waiting to going downstairs." This time, Weisman waited for Hoover to respond.

Silence.

"Is that clear?"

"Perfectly." Hoover replied. The line went dead.

Weisman replaced the receiver gently and rose from his chair to recover the stamp.

He closed his eyes and contemplated the names and faces on his staff. No one stood out as a likely suspect, but there must be a snitch in the crowd.

His parting words came back to haunt him. He told Hoover that Rory's article was on his desk ready to go to print.

Was that a mistake?

He would know when he arrived at his office tomorrow morning.

# Chapter 10

After the interview, I went back to my apartment, climbed into bed, and pulled the covers over my head.

I woke up from a troubled sleep around midnight, starving and with a headache from hell. I stared into my refrigerator praying it would suddenly manifest a meal. I waited for a miracle to occur, then faced reality: a trip to the all night diner on Vermont Avenue was necessary if I was not going to starve. I grabbed my wallet and keys and took along Marilyn's journal.

There were plenty of window tables available at Duke's Diner. I opened the notebook wondering if it was more poems or a diary. The cover read: *Notes: January 1959 – May 1960.* I thumbed through it. There was a section on the birth of the Renaissance in northern Italy. In Marilyn's distinguished hand, it read:

Medici 1400AD – 1748
Prototype first type
Giovanni di Bicci first founding home
Bronze doors in the baptistery
In Florence 1424
Ghiberti 23 perspective
Used his great architect Brunelleschi 22
Donatello 1386 – 1466
Masaccio 1401 – 1428
Father of modern art (reality, poverty careless about his life
But not his painting)
Giovanni di Bicci responsible for him.

His work never recognized until after his death.
The Pantheon – temple in Rome
Greek philosophy – the Golden Mean
(neither too big – or too small)
Ousted, old Pope
Gave money for temples to Brunelleschi
Elected him Signoria (president)
Gonfaloniere (governing body)

Grande – nobles
Geovanni di Bicci – 1428
*

Cosimo (Pater Patriae)
1424 – first public library
Pietro ------------------Giovani
Lorenzo -----------------Giuliano
(the magnificent)
Machiavelli (1469 – 1527)
Botticelli

Right below this intellectual curiosity was one of her casual observations.

New York feb 24
Too young to be so sad—
Slender trees feeling the pangs of growth.

She was ever the poet.

Marilyn Monroe was a person in deep conflict. The sexy movie star that men around the globe, and probably many women, dreamed of taking to bed, was in reality a bookish scholar who would feel more at home in a research library than she does blown up on the screen.

Thinking it over, I felt that my first instincts were correct: I had crept too close to the fire of her psyche and she pulled back, aware that she'd confided too much about herself to a complete stranger. Who could blame her?

For the next two hours, I sat like an image in an Edward Hopper painting. I got back to my apartment just in time to shower, shave, and down a gallon of coffee before going to face Weisman.

My natural tendency toward insecurity on this, my first real job, was convincing me I might be fired for how I handled the interview.

Marilyn left in a huff. Had she already called the paper to complain?

# Chapter 11

It was eight a.m. Time to catch the bus.

As I closed the front door, I jolted. Something was missing. Then it hit me. My folder on the Black Dahlia wasn't on the dining table where I'd left it when I went for the interview. I was sure I'd brought it home Friday night. I stood in the doorway for a minute to review the past couple of days. Nothing stood out.

There'd been so much flying around in my pea-brain I couldn't remember every detail. I handed in my Dahlia article Saturday morning to Weisman in his office. Maybe I left the folder on his desk? With all the non-stop activity his week, I'm surprised I remembered to put on my boxer shorts.

The morning bus was packed and a strange odor hung about. As we bumped our way down Wall Street, I only had one thing on my mind: buy a car. I wanted a convertible so I could feel the wind in my face. I had daydreams of wandering aimlessly through side streets in the Wilshire District on quiet, Sunday afternoons.

The minute I stepped foot into the newsroom, Carol waved her arms frantically to get my attention. She pointed toward the boss's office. There were already five cigarette butts in his ashtray. Carol closed the door and locked it.

Weisman smiled the type of smile someone brandishes when they are about to tell you something you'd rather not hear. My mind raced through the possibilities. "What's going on, have we been robbed?"

Weisman stubbed out a smoke. "That depends." He shot a glance at Carol. She peered through the mail slot of the door, then turned around and gave the all-clear sign.

Weisman leaned back in his chair, hands behind his head, staring up at the ceiling. "When we parted company on Saturday morning after you dropped off your Dahlia article, do you recall if it was on my desk when you left?"

It only took a second for me to respond. "Yes, it was."

Weisman straightened back up. "You're sure about that?"

"Absolutely." This was making me nervous. I felt like I was in an episode of *Perry Mason*.

"Has it disappeared? Because if it has, it might be with my folder."

Carol and Weisman gave each other an insider's look. Carol spoke. "You missing something too?"

They stared at me. "Yeah, well, I mean, I think so. I took home some notes on the Dahlia case Friday night. I left the file on my dining table before I went to interview Marilyn yesterday, but when I got home at seven o'clock, it was gone. I thought maybe I'd left it here and just forgot."

Weisman to Carol: "Go through the kid's desk—but I'm sure it's not there."

My anxiety grew. The boss hadn't asked me how my interview with Monroe went; that subject seemed to be tabled for the moment. I was ready to explode. Carol returned shaking her head no with a nervous quickness.

Weisman excused her. She left the office. When the door clicked shut, he offered me a cigarette. I took a pass.

He lit up. "I'm sure an American history buff like yourself knows who's in charge of what branch of any particular sector of our Federal Government, am I right?"

I nodded.

"Well, then the name, J. Edgar Hoover, and his Federal Bureau of Investigation should be somewhat familiar to you?"

I replied. "Sure, but…"

Weisman waved me off. "The big man called me yesterday afternoon while you were making eyes at Monroe. He asked me to take you off the Black Dahlia and give you another assignment. He knew, and I can't figure out how, that Rory Daniel Long was digging up old dirt, looking for new plant life in the barren desert of that unsolved case."

Weisman paused to search my face. "Now, only three people knew that I'd given you this assignment: myself, Carol, and you. I can eliminate Carol and myself from spilling the beans, but I don't know you well enough to assume that you didn't blab about it to someone." He blew a smoke ring. "So, now's the time bub—did you, or didn't you, mention your assignment to anyone?"

I wasn't offended. I could sense his fear. "I swear, with God as my witness, I haven't even seen a friend or neighbor since you gave me the job. I've been completely swamped with preparing for the interview and working on the Dahlia article at my apartment or here, in the office."

Weisman perked up. "During this week, when you were at your desk working, did you leave your notes out when you got a cup of coffee or took a pee? Anything like that?"

I smiled. "Guilty, your honor. I never cover up my work when I leave my desk for a few minutes. I'm sorry if that was a mistake."

Weisman smiled back. "Hell no, you didn't do anything wrong, but now I have a much clearer picture." He quickly changed subjects. "So, how was your afternoon with the Goddess?"

I brandished a Cheshire-cat grin. "Well, it beat the shit out of watching Freddie Blassey and Mr. Moto on channel five pro-wrestling."

I stayed with Weisman until lunchtime, recounting my afternoon at the Polo Lounge. I had my notes with me. I read examples of Marilyn's poetry, her philosophic quips, and some of the excerpts from her journal, along with as much of our conversation as possible. I felt her love of the Italian Renaissance sparked her intellectual side.

The *Herald* could tell her fans worldwide, that Marilyn Monroe had an exceptional brain with the curiosity and dedication of a scholar.

I didn't tell Weisman about Marilyn's abrupt departure. I still wasn't confident enough to know if I had handled the interview well or not. I thought that there was still a chance she might call to complain.

So far, so good.

Weisman seemed to be somewhere else. I didn't think he was listening when he broke his silence and launched into a pep talk. "Sounds great, kiddo, I'm sure that you'll write a great series of articles. You're doing all the right things and she seems to be responding." He pointed a finger at me. "Tell me, where did you stash the triplicate copy of the Dahlia article?"

I'd forgotten I'd done that. "Oh, right…that's locked up in my desk drawer along with Marilyn's phone number."

Weisman motioned with his head, and we went to my desk. He smiled. "Got that key handy?"

I reached into my jacket pocket and pulled it out.

"Go ahead." Weisman surveilled the news room slowly as I opened the drawer. The triplicate copy was there along with Marilyn's phone number.

"All present and accounted for, chief."

He took the copy while looking around the room. He spoke without looking at me. "That's great. Now keep her number with you and write it down somewhere that you feel is safe and secure, other than this drawer."

I knew there was more going on than I was told. "Anything I can do to help out?"

Weisman returned to himself. "You could bring me a corned beef on rye with some deli pickles, and a cream soda from Nat's when you return from lunch." His face was all smiles. "And also, you could buy yourself a suit of armor. You may need it in the next few days."

He patted me on the shoulder. "Get me a rough draft of the first installment of your interview with Marilyn by tomorrow." He grabbed his chin as though musing, then broke his trance and shooed me out of the newsroom like I was five years old, waving his arms and stomping his feet.

I ran out shouting over my shoulder: "One corned beef on rye coming up."

# Chapter 12

The bus ride home from work took forever. Sometimes it's not good to have a lot of time to think things over.

I have always felt cheated by my grandfather's death.

I came into the world two years after he was buried. My grandmother did her best to fill the void left by her husband, taking over his responsibilities politically and socially, but, by the time I was able to understand adult conversation, she was out of the game and rarely did she speak of the past. I was brooding over these thoughts while sorting through my notes from my interview with Marilyn.

Weisman told me that my piece on Liz Short's murder might not be published un-edited. Hoover lowered the boom. Weisman had defied Hoover's order and was printing my article in one form or another, but would it have any impact? I wondered.

I heated up a Swanson's T.V. dinner and continued organizing. I needed to call Marilyn in the morning to arrange returning her journal. Maybe there was a chance we might meet again. Maybe she'll invite me to come over for a swim and lunch around the swimming pool. Maybe I should have my head examined.

At ten thirty, I went for a walk around the neighborhood for a half-hour or so, hoping it might help me get to sleep. When I put my key in the door, the phone was ringing. I raced in thinking it might be my mother. All I could hear was the sounds of a wild party. Jazz was being played full bore, and there was laughter in the background, accompanied by muffled voices. I screamed hello, but there was no response. Then I heard a very faint voice call my name.

"Rory?"

"…Marilyn, is that you?" She'd asked me for my phone number at the Polo Lounge. I never dreamed she'd use it.

Her voice came back stronger. "Yes, Rory, it's me." She giggled. She sounded high on something. The music was fading. She was on the move. I heard a door slam. All was quiet.

Marilyn cooed her words. 'Oh, Rory, I'm so sorry for the way I left you yesterday. But I just had to go. I realized today that I was trying to escape from myself."

She cupped her hand over the phone, her muffled voice undistinguishable. She was talking with someone who had entered the room. She said a few words to whoever. I waited—she returned. "Where do you live, Rory?"

I looked at the clock. It was eleven-thirty. This can't be happening. "I live at the Bronson Arms in Silver Lake. It's known as East Hollywood. It's the area where the first silent film studios were located before Hollywood came to be." Jesus Christ, I sound like one of those fucking idiots on a Beverly Hills bus tour with a megaphone.

"May I have your address? Would it be okay if I came to see you for a while? I have a cab waiting right now."

I tried to be levelheaded. "Well, I don't know. Where are you? Are you in Hollywood, or…?"

She cut me off. "I'm in Santa Monica—I'll be there in twenty minutes." She whispered.

"But I will need your address."

I nearly peed in my pants. I stammered out my location. She hung up.

Okay. Marilyn Monroe has just told you she's on her way over. Now, what's the first thing to do? *Panic!*

There was a light drizzle as the yellow cab trudged its way along Venice Boulevard, closing in on midnight. A summer rain had surprised the city of angels.

In the back seat, the lady wore huge sunglasses. Her black, curly locks sprouted out beneath a canvas fisherman's hat. She stared out the window at the storefronts, which lined the sidewalks, absorbed in thought.

Marilyn sobered up along the drive. The cab hung a left onto La Cienega, off Venice Boulevard, and three minutes later, made a right onto Beverly. Now it was a straight line to East Hollywood.

She spotted a phone booth and asked the driver to pull over. She dialed Rory's number. He picked up. She hung up and went back to the cab. "No," she told herself, "I mustn't be a coward." Her current shrink told her that one of her big problems was fear—that she was afraid of life and that being a movie idol offered her distance from people.

The cabbie wasn't a talker like most of them. She felt strangely at peace with herself, secure in the moment. She was a good judge of character, and Rory was at the top of the list. She could usually depend on her intuition to guide her. Unfortunately, her intuition could be manipulated by a certain kind of man: at least that's how it'd been up to this point.

Rain fell gently as the windshield wipers danced a slow ballet. The swish of tires gliding through the wet streets was hypnotic. Her soul settled. She was able to talk to herself and receive clear answers. The darkened silence forced her to ask a very important question.

Why did she feel compelled to be with Rory Long, a young man she barely knew? She bit her lower lip while concentrating. He was safe. He was young and innocent, and she felt he respected her. She could go to him at midnight and feel secure in his company. And, in truth, it was a matter of getting away from the party before she did something she might regret. She had mixed barbiturates and alcohol—not the best combination. Men were jockeying for position to take advantage of her.

They crossed Vermont Avenue traveling along Beverly Boulevard until it merged with Silver Lake Boulevard. The cabbie announced, "Bronson Arms is on the right, ma'am." He checked his meter.

"That'll be seven dollars and fifty-three cents, please."

Marilyn handed him a ten and told him to keep the change.

For a split second, he thought he recognized her. "Nah, it couldn't be."

It was just past midnight.

I sat on the couch staring at the yellow street lamp, thinking that I'd dreamed the whole thing up, when there were three light taps on my front door.

I opened it to find the Marilyn looking like she did when she arrived at the Polo Lounge. She entered quickly. No words were exchanged. She was immediately drawn to my bookcase, leaning forward and perusing the titles before she said hello.

"Well, Rory, we meet again." Her laugh was natural. She'd sobered up since her call.

I stood off to the side with my hands stuffed into my trouser pockets like a kid waiting for his mother to offer him a candy bar... pathetic. "Yep, here we are, except we are here, in my place."

She removed her disguise. The transformation was unreal. Beneath the image of a homeless old woman was the gorgeous, stunning Marilyn Monroe as the public knows and adores her. She shimmered in a black, tightly-fit cocktail dress accessorized by a necklace of opaque pearls that was probably worth more than my salary for a year. She looked at herself in the mirror over my fireplace and fluffed her hair. When she turned around, I almost passed out. I could kick myself for not owning a camera.

She smiled with her entire body. 'Well, aren't you going to offer a lady a drink?"

I'm not sure where this fault in men comes from. I was as nervous as Tom Ewell in *The Seven Year Itch*. What is it about a beautiful woman that causes a man to melt before their very eyes? I stammered, hee-hawed, and basically made a fool of myself darting around and trying to locate a bottle of bourbon that was right in front of my bookcase, on a serving tray, complete with two tumblers.

Of course, Marilyn picked up on my inexperience.

Ann Frank could have.

She stood with a swaggered hip and pointed towards the booze. "Maybe this will do?" Another laugh on me, or for me, I couldn't determine which.

I poured us each a half tumbler, and of course spilled some in the process, further adding to my clumsiness. Without direction, we sat on my small divan and toasted each other at quarter past midnight. Now I knew I was dreaming.

Marilyn seemed lost in thought for a few moments as if she were catching up with herself at day's end, or should I say, day's beginning. "Wait a minute. I brought something with me tonight even though I had no idea I'd end up here with you. Isn't it funny how things turn out? I mean, how we create fate by setting things subconsciously in motion?"

I had no idea where this was going. She jumped off the couch and grabbed her coat. She withdrew a journal from the inside pocket. She was already opening the cover as she sat back down, this time closer to me.

I remembered that I had one of her journals from yesterday, but I was too overwhelmed by her presence to think about handing it to her.

"In nineteen-fifty-five, I returned to New York to study with Lee. The studio paid for my room at the Waldorf-Astoria." She grinned. "I used to call it the Waldorf-Hysteria because there was so much partying going on in those days."

That dreamy look came over her.

"I used to love to stand on my terrace, which was really just a part of the roof way up high." Marilyn touched my shoulder, and I almost exploded. "You know, Rory, when you're very high up in one of those sky-scrapers in Manhattan, looking down, you feel...I don't know...you feel like you own the world. Everything inside of you changes for a few moments."

I nodded my head up and down like one of those dashboard mechanical pets: a dog, or cat, responding to the car's movement. I was so sure that she could finally see me for what I am: a young, middle-class working jerk who got lucky. Sitting in my apartment, sharing a drink with the most recognized woman on the planet, I felt like a hoax, a charlatan—someone who had entered a cathedral without knowing how to cross himself.

Marilyn picked up on my mood. "You know, Rory, I have never shown these poems to anyone, not even Arthur." Marilyn put her arm around my shoulders like a coach comforting a player. "I trust you. I just know that you'll tell my story the way I want it to be, even if at this moment you're not sure how you are going to explain me to the world."

She squeezed me. "That's why I called you. Even in the short time I've known you, I feel I can count on you."

I was completely under her spell. She could have asked me to walk off a cliff, and I would have done so, no questions asked.

With her arm still in place, and my left leg touching her right, she locked eyes with me and slowly moved her lips toward mine.

It was half past midnight, and the city was still, not even the sound of a passing car.

She tapped my lips with the first finger of her left hand, smiled, and then kissed me: a gentle, slow kiss sustained for a few moments, then withdrawn.

I'd like to say that it was different than any kiss I'd shared in the past, but it wasn't. It was just a kiss, but after her lips left mine and she straightened up on the couch, something snapped. If I had been an Arthurian Knight of the Round Table, and Lady Guinevere had just bestowed her scarf on me, it couldn't have matched the feeling that surged through my body. It could be described as a ball of energy, but it was much, much more.

I felt as if I had arrived somewhere, at a destination I wasn't aware I was traveling to.

Marilyn poured two more shots of bourbon and went back to her journal. "Now, let's read some of these poems and see if they're any good."

I could have died and gone to heaven. There was really no reason to do anything else in my life. No amount of visceral experience could match this moment in time. I viewed her with a different set of eyes. I asked her to recite some of her poems. We clinked our tumblers, took a sip, and she began:

Now, this moment is mine,
and it's gone.
Some swift memory

speeding away.
I felt as though
I could hold on,
But no, it left me.

The poem felt electric. It was the mirror image of the kiss. She kept on reading. I sat quietly, taking notes without making a sound with my pen on the paper. I listened to her for about twenty minutes. This was the last poem.

Lights in the darkness,
Buildings overpowering life.
What was yesterday's thought?
It seems as far away as the moon-
As a child I could not understand,
The river - made of soda-pop -
the park full of candy trees.
These things I don't see:
I'm looking at my lover
Like the moon as a child.

When she finished, her body sank into the couch as if someone had dumped her there. I called out her name, but she had faded fast. I lit a cigarette and pulled my legs underneath me. I wondered if she ever got any real sleep. Jesus Christ, Marilyn Monroe is asleep on my couch.

Who in the hell would believe it?

It was nearly two a.m. when I finished my cigarette. An uncontrollable yawn accompanied by a weird groaning sound came out of me. She stirred. Perfect. That's all I would need in my box of memories. "Remember the time you belched and woke up Marilyn Monroe?"

I went to fetch a quilt. When I returned, she had kicked her shoes off and was stretched out with a pillow under her head. Her breathing was slow and even. I covered her with the blanket and sat near her, watching her breasts heave to the pulse of her breathing: so slow, so soothing, so sexy.

Time for beddy-bye for this kid.

As I buttoned my pajamas, I pictured the kiss. I was so exhausted I couldn't sleep. I sat in bed with my notes and continued to write. Words flowed out of my pen effortlessly, but there was a problem.

As hard as I tried, I couldn't resist sexual desire, fueled by my imagination. I was so tempted to go and peel back the quilt, very slowly, allowing my eyes to travel along her incredible body. Even fully clothed she gave me a hard-on; her perfume wafted into my bedroom—Damnit! The intellect can only carry you so far into those lofty clouds. Sooner or later, your libido takes charge.

I'm not sure when I fell asleep.

The alarm clock went off at seven a.m. I leapt out of bed and ran into the living room. She was gone. I never heard her leave. I had no idea when she did.

Still in a deep fog, I scanned the room looking for signs of her. I was just spaced enough to think I'd dreamed the whole thing up.

The liquor caddy was back in place. The bottle, which was full when Marilyn arrived, was now half gone. This was the first evidence I had to validate my memory. The tumblers had been washed and dried and set neatly back in their place. The quilt was folded on the couch.

I blinked my eyes several times, trying to figure out if I was awake or back in a dream. My legs gave way and I fell onto the couch. When I landed, I spotted an envelope on the coffee table. I hesitated to touch it. If it disappeared before my eyes, I would know I made all of this up.

The stationery was from the Bel-Air Hotel. My name was handwritten on the front. I needed a coffee desperately, but this couldn't wait. Her Chanel No. 5 lingered.

I took a deep breath, timidly removing the note from the envelope.

*Dear Rory,*

*I hope that you don't think less of me after my impromptu visit last night. I'm sorry to leave without saying goodbye, but that was what I had to do. It's not easy being me. I am always chasing my own shadow.*

*Thank you for a wonderful evening, we'll talk soon. Let me know about your progress on my article.*

*Sincerely,*
*Marilyn*

*Ps. your couch is very comfy – that's the first decent sleep I've had in months.*

I desperately needed coffee and a smoke.

It was just dawning on me what had taken place in the past forty-eight hours:

I spent Sunday afternoon chatting with Marilyn Monroe at one of the most exclusive bars in Hollywood, and the following night, she phoned to see if it was alright for her to stop by 'round Midnight for a drink, and within thirty minutes of her arrival, she kissed me and ended up spending the night. These facts force me to ask the same question again:

Who in the hell would believe it?

I tripped over my own feet racing for the stove. I rounded the corner and slid along the wood floor in my slippers. I sped past the dining table and almost had a heart attack. There sat my Dahlia folder, right where I'd left it. Of course, it didn't just get up and walk away; someone took it and then returned it.

This was creepy. Why would anyone do that?

After Weisman put the fear of God into me concerning J. Edgar and his crew, I became even more paranoid. My thoughts momentarily left Marilyn to ponder the mystery of my disappearing file: did the FBI take it, or should I say, borrow it to copy it? So why would they even think about returning it—what was the point? Was this their way of scaring me off? If that's the case, their plan was working.

One thought kept hammering home: *Why?*

The bus ride to work went by in a flash. I found a nineteen fifty-seven Chevrolet, convertible, from a private party. The owner was bringing it for me to see at end of the day.

Normally, I would have been drooling in anticipation of having the car of my dreams by this evening, but my thoughts kept drifting back to Marilyn.

On this Tuesday morning, time didn't exist. Memory recaptured every move she made from the moment she stepped inside my apartment.

In the deep quiet that occurs when emotions run high, I began to think that her kiss was a test. If I'd climbed all over her, she may have left on the spot, never to call again. What the hell am I thinking? She may never call again anyway. Why would she?

There was that *why* again.

# Chapter 13

The boss was not in his office. Carol was also absent. I called down to the print room to see if Tom knew where they were. He had no idea.

My Dahlia article was set to go. I was sure Weisman had taken the blue pencil to it. I wasn't happy about that, but I understood. Hoover applied pressure, and Weisman could only push back so hard.

I sat typing up my notes on Marilyn. I'd only had a chance to say hello, or "how-ya-doin'" to the other journalists on the floor in the short time I'd been here. I didn't really have any friends I could grab a coffee with and find out what's going on, so I continued to plow away, "waiting for Godot."

Close to the noon hour the pair strolled in. They paused at the switchboard, sharing a laugh with the operator. Weisman headed for his office waving for me to join him, sporting a big grin.

Now what?

Carol acted strange as I passed her. I said hello, but she didn't respond. She headed for her desk with an expression I couldn't define: was it a warm, happy glow, or a warning against an oncoming storm?

I gave the door a gentle rap.

"Enter, young fellow, my lad, as the British might put it. Come in and take a load off."

The editor was smiling from ear to ear as if he had just won the Irish sweepstakes. Dead center on his desk was the article I had left Saturday morning, which had just as mysteriously disappeared and re-appeared as my file folder. I blurted out, "My article got returned also?"

Weisman perked up. "Inferring that your file folder made it home after being kidnapped?"

I nodded in confirmation.

He stood to stretch. "You know something, my friend, I've been in this business for over thirty years, and thought I'd seen damn near everything. But then you came to work for the *Examiner*."

He sat back down hurriedly and picked up an envelope sitting next to my article, turning it over and over. It was a heavy manila type, often used for photos. His eyes darted back and forth from the envelope to me. Finally, he said. "Curious as to what might be in this baby?" He dropped it on his desk. It made a heavy thud sound.

He changed his mood and the subject. The smile was gone. "So, tell me, whad'ya do last night—stay home to write up your interview with everybody's favorite tits and ass?"

That comment pissed me off. Weisman was my boss, but I'd be damned if he was going to talk about her like that. He didn't know her; I did. He didn't spend a few hours listening to her share her feelings about the world around her; I did.

"Excuse me, sir, but I think you're a little bit out of line. She doesn't deserve to be referred to that way. She's really a good person, warm and gentle."

The ear-to-ear smile returned. "Oh, is she now? And I'm out of line, am I? Well, what the hell, you should know, my friend. My, oh my, how we've grown up in the past few days." He laid into me. "Listen to me, you little shit—you should have called me the minute Monroe phoned you last night."

I was shocked. How did he know about that? What else did he know?

Weisman's face was turning red. He hit a switch on his com-box. "Carol, get in here on the double." Within seconds, she arrived with a stack of papers, setting them out in three neat rows on the desk.

My heart stuck in my throat.

Weisman dumped out the contents of the manila envelope. A pile of eight-by-ten, black-and-white, grainy photos, taken through an open window of my apartment, stared up at me from the top of his desk. The first one that caught my eye was Marilyn and me sharing a drink on the couch. In a state of panic, I shuffled through the stack, and my biggest fear came true: there were three close-ups of our kiss and a final shot of me putting the quilt on her as she slept.

I felt faint. What the fuck had I done? I had no idea there were spies lurking in the bushes outside my apartment. I shrank in my chair.

Carol stood behind Weisman to offer a friendly face, but I was too shocked to believe she was sincere.

Weisman was steaming.

I didn't know what to say. I tried to defend myself against the undefinable. "I…just couldn't believe that she'd called me. Everything happened so fast. The next thing I knew she was at my front door, and then…she just came in and, well, we had a drink and she read me some of her poems."

Weisman burst out in a maniacal laugh. "Oh, so it was an evening of culture. Did you both recite from T.S. Eliot? Maybe your favorite verses from *The Wasteland*?" He pounded his fist so hard on the desk, that the ashtray rattled off and crashed onto the floor, spilling a dozen butts as it shattered.

"Do you have any idea what a mess you've made for the paper?" Carol cleaned up as Weisman came around his desk to face me. "Don't you see that whoever took these shots and graciously offered them for our perusal is more than likely prepared to wall-paper the world with them?"

Jesus, what had I done?

All I did was answer my phone. How would anyone else react if Marilyn Monroe called and invited herself over for a visit? The more I thought about it, my anxiety began to fade away. The confrontational side of my family's genetic pool suddenly kicked in. I stood up and got right into Weisman's face. Mere millimeters separated us.

Confidence took over.

"Well, what the fuck is the big deal anyway? You can kick me off this two-bit, rag of a paper if you want to, but all I did last night was answer my phone when a friend called and told me she were coming over for a visit. Okay, this friend happens to be famous, but since when has J. Edgar made that against the law, if that's whom you're worrying about? Is it? Or isn't it?

"And, quite frankly, Mr. Weisman, I can't believe you're so naïve as to think that the most popular female film star in the history of cinema is going to get kicked out of tinsel-town because she offered a twenty-five-year-old goofball a kiss on the lips, more than likely, because she felt so goddamn sorry for his raggedy ass."

I was on a roll.

"Maybe, just maybe, you could sit your tired and experienced ass back down in that chair and call upon whatever brain cells you've got left to figure out a way to make this event work for the paper instead of worrying about an innocent event, which could just as easily be interpreted as an affectionate moment between consenting adults!"

I was drenched in sweat. My weight pulled me back into the chair. My eyes were closed, and I was out of breath. When I looked up, Weisman was seated back behind his desk, contemplating me with his fingertips touching in church-steeple fashion, elbows on his stomach.

Carol was still behind him. She gave me the thumbs up thinking he couldn't see it. "That'll be all for now, Carol, you're excused." Carol made a beeline for the door and exited in under three seconds.

He spoke when my breathing became natural. "I'll need you to sign these papers for our legal department. It relieves the paper from any actions that may be taken against you, by any, and all parties because of last night's incident. It states that you were acting on your own volition and were not under instructions of any kind from me or any other member of the *Examiner* family, concerning the rendezvous with Ms. Monroe." When he finished, he held up a pen.

At this point, I felt I had nothing to lose. "You don't mind if I read the documents before deciding whether or not to sign them, do you?"

Weisman took one sheet from each stack. "Be my guest, but there is no *if* available here. You will need to sign them if you want to keep your job."

I was taken aback. "I'm sorry…you said what? You're not going to fire me if I designate myself as the person responsible for any, and all fall out, concerning Ms. Monroe's visit to my apartment last night?" I paused to let my statement sink in. "Am I clear on this?"

Weisman's business smile returned. "That's about it, kiddo. You sign these papers and your job is secure. Don't get me wrong. You fucked up big time. But I can chalk that up to inexperience. I don't think you did anything intentionally against the paper, but the big cheese upstairs wants no part of defending you, if, and when accusations are filed against you about your time spent with the little lady." Weisman paused to shuffle through the photos, shaking his head back and forth.

"And I'm telling you, son, when these photos get circulated, there's no telling where things will go. I predict lots of flack heading your way." His business smile returned as he held up the ballpoint pen. "At least we can protect your job at the paper." He motioned with the pen in the air for me to take it while continuing his fatherly image.

Now, I leaned back in my chair and church-steepled my fingers. My family DNA was in full possession. "Well, who in the hell thinks I give a shit about staying with this organization?"

Weisman's dropped the pin and his smile. He wasn't ready for this. He was counting on me begging to keep my job. I lit a cigarette for effect. Now that the ashtray was in pieces in the trash, I threw the match on the floor. I picked up the stack of photos, shoving back the unsigned documents.

"Say, that's a nice shot of us toasting each other. I might have this blown up into poster size. And this one shot of our kissing, say, that's a real winner." I plopped the stack of photos on his desk.

"Allan…" I flicked an ash, "my gut feeling is that any magazine from *Look* to *Reader's Digest* would give an arm and a leg for an article written by the young newspaper journalist who ends up spending a night with Marilyn Monroe in his apartment at her request." My confidence was showing. "I would guess that a sizeable check would accompany my efforts to describe, with the greatest accuracy and in fine detail, the events of the evening. This article would probably give me enough money to take my time in regards to any decision which I may ponder regarding my immediate future." I got excited. "Wow, I'll bet the book advance alone would give me a few years of financial independence to really think things through."

Weisman sat perfectly still.

"So, boss—we're at a stalemate unless you can come up with a better offer than letting me be tarred and feathered while you and the big shots continue with your two hour, twenty-five-dollar, two-dry-martini lunches." I finished my smoke and stomped it out on the floor.

Weisman didn't react. He stared at me in a meditative manner as he reached over to his com-box. "Carol, we need a fresh ashtray in here, and call the grill at the Regent and have lunch sent up to my office for Rory and me." He cupped the phone, blinking his eyes rapidly in a comedic fashion. "You okay with medium-rare, Rory?"

I nodded.

"Two New York Fillets, medium rare. Thanks." He released the button. "Okay, pal, let's you and I have a talk." He hit the button again. "Oh, and Carol, have them send round a pitcher of dry martinis also."

I didn't have a chance to take my jacket off when I arrived at Weisman's office. I had sweated through my shirt during our shouting match.

Wiseman told me he needed to make some calls before our lunch. He'd signal me when lunch arrived.

I grabbed a spare shirt kept in my desk and headed for the men's room. Walking down the hall, the title of a W.C. Field's movie I caught on television the other night came to me:

*Never Give a Sucker an Even Break.*

# Chapter 14

After toweling down, I returned to my desk and stared at the phone. I knew Weisman would have a heart attack if I called Marilyn, but I needed to know she was okay, even if she was pissed off. I knew I only had a few minutes at the most before lunch was wheeled in. I dialed. She picked up.

Her voice was subdued. "Hello...?"

I jumped in. "Marilyn, its Rory—don't yell at me. I had no idea that there were photographers prowling around outside my apartment last night...I'm so sorry..."

She hadn't heard one word I'd said. "Rory, what time is it? What day is it? I've just returned from a long trip. There are stars on the ceiling above my bed. I can see the entire universe from here."

She was stoned. I had to move fast. She didn't seem aware of the photos. Out of the corner of my eye, I spied the waiter with the cart. "Listen, I have to go, call me when you get the chance, if you want to, or can, or... The food cart was at the office door. "Call me! Bye."

I hung up as Weisman stepped out of his office to wave me over. As a backup for a meeting of which I had no idea of the outcome, I took the rough first draft of what I'd typed so far on Marilyn.

When I entered, the waiter poured me a martini. I sat down and tucked my tie into my shirt.

Weisman raised his glass. He motioned for me to pick up mine. "Here's to bigger and better crime so that we have something shocking to tell the world every day of our lives." He smiled and nearly drained half of his extra-dry ambrosia.

I sipped mine. The waiter pulled the dome-metal covers off our plates, and there sat two charbroiled steaks, baked potatoes, and veggies... rolls, butter, fine cutlery, the works, including linen napkins.

Weisman smiled. "*Bon appetite*, as they say in France."

Few words were exchanged as we ate.

I was so full of anxiety that I could hardly taste anything. With every bite, I was expecting him to come unglued after the tongue-lashing I gave him less than an hour ago. To my surprise, he remained placid, occasionally commenting on the food.

When we finished, he offered me another martini. I declined. He poured one for himself. I took a coffee. We both lit up and leaned back in our chairs. He hit his com-box and someone came in to clear away the tray. He stared at me as if he were putting his thoughts in order. I waited, thinking time had stood still.

"You know, Rory, I made a few phone calls around this great nation of ours before lunch." He pushed the brand new ashtray into the center of his desk with a wry smile. "It's very interesting because no one else has these photos. Not our local competitors, not New York. In fact, I checked with the associated press and they had no idea what I was talking about." We flicked our ashes at the same time. "So, what does that tell us, young man?"

I was stumped. In the few seconds that I had this information, I couldn't find rhyme or reason for the photos to be exclusively in our hands.

Having no solution, I responded with a question. "Maybe enough time hasn't past. When the photos arrived this morning, were they hand-delivered by a messenger? Can anyone describe this person?"

Weisman took a long drag on his cigarette and another sip of his second martini. "I'm afraid there are no witnesses to the drop-off. The photos were on the receptionist's desk when she arrived, with my name on the cover along with *confidential* stamped in red ink." He paused to check my reaction. "This isn't a Charlie Chan movie, my young friend. We can't get number two son to check all the typewriters to find the one that has a raised *h*."

Weisman stood and began to pace around the office. "The first thing we should be asking ourselves is *why?*"

That sounded familiar.

He continued. "Now, why should someone, or a group, go to the trouble to take candid, revealing photos of a superstar in the arms of an unknown yutz from Jersey?" He waved a hand.

"Don't take offence, son, that's just a saying we use in the business. There is obviously a reason, there has to be. But what reason? Is the portfolio to be used as a leverage of some kind when the party responsible wants a favor or two from the paper?"

I had an idea. "Maybe it's one of the fan magazines? They probably have photographers following her all the time. When she left in the cab for my place, they just did what they're paid to do. Maybe they're waiting for the right time to plaster the magazine stands with a photo spread of Marilyn and her new *yutz* of a lover?"

Weisman laughed as he pulled out the three legal papers that I had declined to sign earlier.

"Listen, kid, you might not be that far off. Just do me a fucking favor and sign these damn things so I can get administration off our backs, then you and I can put our heads together and try to figure this out."

He dropped the pen he was about to hand me. He smiled warmly. "You were right earlier today, as much as I hate to admit it. From day one, I've always thought that Marilyn Monroe was pure class. But believe me, kiddo, there's a lot that has gone on behind the scenes that you don't know about."

He paused to check my reaction. I didn't offer one.

"She's been around the world a few times, if you get my drift, and I'm not being disrespectful. I'm thrilled with the attitude you have toward her: believe me, you're one privileged son-of-a-bitch to have gotten so close to her." He held up his hand apologetically. "No disrespect intended for your mother!"

I took a pen and signed the papers. He tucked them away the second I did.

I had mixed feelings about Allan Weisman.

Part of me didn't trust him. But the part that did also respected him. Some inner voice told me to ride this event to the finish line. I had said my piece, and if, by any chance, these photos showed up somewhere else, I would still have the options. That is, if I were still breathing.

I had to admit that a sense of fear followed me around. The missing, then returned file, and now the spies who took the photos were adding to the weight of what was already a pretty hefty paranoia.

I took off my jacket and loosened my tie.

Weisman looked up. From out of nowhere, he asked, "How was your steak?"

The query caught me by surprise. "Great, and thanks, that really hit the spot."

He seemed to be in a trance. I waited for him to return. "I'm wondering if these photos are more directed at you than everyone's favorite blonde." Weisman massaged his chin. "What if there's a political faction that found out the grandson of Huey Long was working here? They may have been originally tracking Marilyn, then you arrived on the scene and...?"

The forty-eight-year-old newsman leaned back and rubbed his eyes. He looked aged beyond his years. "Oh, I don't know—none of this makes any sense.

Why in the hell would someone go to the trouble to take these shots and then sit on them after delivering them to us?"

I must have had the most frightened look on my face.

Weisman studied me for a few moments, then proudly announced, "Welcome to the club, kid."

# Chapter 15

The woman burst into Marilyn's bedroom without knocking and violently pulled back the curtains on the windows facing east. Sunlight streaked across the bed as the star grappled with a pillow, pulling it over her face.

"There'll be none of that today, missy. Evelyn Welmen gathered up clothes that were scattered all over the floor. She signaled the maid to bring in the breakfast tray. The aroma of fresh coffee and eggs filled the room. It was noon.

Evelyn waved a steaming cup over the bed as if she were performing an exorcism. Marilyn responded like a zombie. She sat up with her eyes closed, arms extended. The woman handed her the coffee. "You've got just thirty minutes, and no more, to pull yourself together." Evelyn paused to let her take a few sips. She knew Monroe wouldn't hear a word said until the caffeine kicked in.

The blonde opened her eyes and looked up. "What day is this?"

A stern reply. "It's been Wednesday for twelve hours now."

She took another sip. "Don't I have something to do today?"

The sixty-two-year-old spinster sighed. She'd been with Marilyn for six months, hired by studio executives to try and keep the megastar from making any irretrievable mistakes in her social life. It wasn't a very easy job. In fact, it was impossible, but the woman had accepted it and she was standing her ground to try and keep the star in line with the universe.

They'd met while filming *The Misfits*. Director John Huston had requested Evelyn to be his script supervisor. It was common knowledge that shooting the movie of Arthur Miller's screenplay would be anything but smooth. Clarke Gable was physically weak: he would pass away two months after the completion of the film. Marilyn was fighting her addiction problems without making any headway. In the end, it was a movie doomed to sag with public favor: it was too damn depressing.

Evelyn had a promising career as a script consultant, gaining praise from such luminaries as Frank Capra, Nunnelly Johnson, and William Wyler. But, she was also one of the unfortunates who had a run-in with Senator McCarthy that cost her a career in the movie business. When she refused to co-operate under oath with his investigation, McCarthy released an article claiming that Evelyn was a lesbian. That was all it took at the time: no proof required. The rumor was enough to silence her telephone. She was officially blacklisted, which meant she could never work in the industry again.

Huston remembered her. He needed someone with Evelyn's experience. He argued with studio heads, tooth and nail, and finally got his way. During the filming of *The Misfits*, Evelyn and Monroe got along well, often taking their breaks together.

When they wrapped the shoot, the higher ups at *Twentieth* offered Welmen a nice salary to become Marilyn Monroe's personal assistant. The star's erratic behavior, due to her drug and alcohol abuse, demanded a watchdog on a twenty-four-hour basis. Evelyn was the perfect choice.

Evelyn watched Marilyn struggle to find which end of the bed sheet offered an exit. The woman smiled that smile a mother exhibits when, after constant reprimands to a problem child, the parent just gives in. She gave in after her first week on the job, just after Marilyn purchased the hacienda-style, single-floor dwelling in Brentwood.

When Evelyn tried to help her set the place up; to arrange what little furniture she possessed, the enigmatic star just wandered off to the garden outside by the pool, completely disinterested. The only object she cared about was her white, baby grand piano. Marilyn called it her *blonde piano*.

The personal assistant could never understand her passion for the instrument. Every time they stayed in a hotel, Marilyn requested one in her suite. In the time she'd been with the star, she'd never seen or heard her play.

Today, the axe was about to fall. George Cukor, one of the world's prominent film directors with over five decades in the business, was due to arrive at the Hacienda to personally give Marilyn her walking papers on his latest film: *Something's Got to Give*, an apropos title. Something did give. Marilyn's film career would soon be on hold.

Evelyn was sorting the mail as Marilyn finished her breakfast. She handed the still sleepy-eyed blonde her robe. "A young man named Rory Long called this morning to say that he'd found one of your journals in a booth at the Polo Lounge. He wanted to return it, so I called the lot in Century City and told them he would be dropping it off sometime this afternoon."

Marilyn perked up. "Rory called? Today—this morning? Why didn't you wake me?"

Evelyn was shocked. "You mean you know this guy? What does he do? Where did you meet him? Is he in the business?"

Marilyn jumped out of bed and headed for the shower. She yelled back at Evelyn. "Cancel all of my appointments and call the *Herald Examiner*. The sleepy star was suddenly full of energy.

"Leave a message for Rory Long to call me this afternoon."

Evelyn raised an eyebrow. "Will do." She set the mail on a nearby table and headed for the living room. First, she called Cukor's office. Fortunately, he was at the studio looking at rushes to see if he could save his movie without Monroe there to complete it.

After making the required calls, Evelyn checked to make sure Marilyn was still in the shower. She then made another call, whispering into the receiver.

# Chapter 16

Weisman sat in his office with the lights off. Neon signs from nearby buildings flickered through the high windows. Dusk descended, inviting the summer sun's slow fade.

It was eight o'clock Wednesday evening. He should have been home by now, two scotches to the good. Fortunately, he thought to call Margaret to let her know he would be working late. He detected the worry in her voice even though she tried to disguise it. They'd been together a long time.

Allan edited Rory's article on the Black Dahlia and sent it downstairs Monday. Due to the fact that the original copy disappeared from his desk, and Rory's file-folder went missing from his apartment, Weisman suspected that the FBI was on the job. Both items were returned. *Careful* would be his by-word from now on.

When Weisman read the article, he admired the passion it contained. He thought back to his beginnings: no difference. Youthful enthusiasm is what it takes to get the wheels turning. Rory began the piece with research taking him in the direction of an unknown suspect, who happened to be a prominent member of the community at the time of the ghastly murder. That information would be left, figuratively, on the cutting-room floor for now.

The experienced editor shaved the corners off Rory's piece without taking away too much punch: just using softer gloves—a few jabs to size up the opponent, saving the knock-out punch for the final round. That is, if the fight wasn't called off.

Hoover had been quite adamant on the phone. Of course, Rory would be upset about his boss doing a clip-job on his research, but Rory was aware of the potential danger involved if the FBI pot boiled over. The kid was learning.

Weisman hadn't moved a muscle in over an hour. His breathing was slow but steady. He had a tough decision to make. He'd checked all day long, every hour on the hour, and still, the photos were a no-show anywhere else.

He needed to make a daring move. It was do-or-die time.

A small bookcase sat behind his desk against the wall. He removed five books from the second shelf to reveal the door of a small wall safe.

He withdrew a red address book. This item contained the phone numbers of prominent persons in the public eye: politicians as well as those in the entertainment field. It had taken him years to compile it.

He opened to the letter H, memorized a number, then put the item back in the safe and replaced the books. His ashtray was full. He lit another cigarette and took a hit of scotch from a small flask he kept for emergencies.

He dialed.

After two rings, a woman's voice answered. "Yes, how may I direct your call?"

Weisman spoke clearly. "I need to speak with Bulldog."

The woman paused before responding casually. "And who may I say is calling?"

"Tell Bulldog, nose-for-news is on the line."

Her voice tightened. "One minute, please."

After enough time to down two more shots for extra courage, Bulldog came on the line.

"Allan, what in the hell do you want? I read the kid's article. Nothing there for us to be concerned with. I would have contacted you by now if there were."

Weisman threw a one-two punch. "What about the photos?"

J. Edgar Hoover squawked, "What photos?"

Weisman responded quickly. "My mistake, sir, I was thinking of something else."

He hung up. He'd won that round. Hoover and his motley crew were not behind the pictures. That sent one contestant away from the ring. Now the problem was that the remaining opponents were masked and could be brass-knuckle fighters.

Was Rory on to something with his theory that one of Hollywood's trash fan magazines might be behind this? Weisman took another hit from his flask and grabbed his coat.

Enough for today.

# Chapter 17

Eleven thirty, Thursday morning. I was zoned in on my article about Marilyn. The phone rang. I needed to finish a sentence before I picked up. After ring number five, I punched line two.

"Rory, you called Tuesday, but I never heard back from you."

Not even a hello. I wasn't sure how to answer. "Um...well, yes and no."

Monroe was cranky. "Listen, Rory Long, you'd better tell me what's going on. Evelyn told me you found one of my journals." Her voice rose in volume. "You've had it since Sunday—you called me back, but before I could say anything, you hung up. It's been two days since then. Why haven't you called?"

Jesus, the woman is upset because Mr. Nobody didn't get in touch with her sooner?

I knew an apology wouldn't cut it. "Yeah, well, a lot has happened since you stopped by Monday night. I should have given it to you while you were there, but my brain shut down. I thought I'd better not let whoever answered your phone know that you'd been here."

"Listen to me! That never happened. Do you hear me? I never came to your apartment. No one must ever know."

Now, what do I do? "Well, someone does know all about it. When I arrived at the paper Tuesday morning, an envelope full of black-and-white photos of you with me, including the kiss, were on Weisman's desk." I thought I was going to have a heart attack. I waited for her response—nothing. "So, you see, keeping this to ourselves is going to be a bit tricky."

Marilyn burst out laughing. It shocked me. She put the phone down. I could hear her in hysterics: insane laughter. She stopped, coughed, and cleared her throat. "Okay, big fellow, we're on a raft in the middle of the Pacific without an oar and no compass." She let out one of her patented giggles. "Come over to my house and bring the journal with you. Can you get the rest of the day off?"

I answered without knowing. "Sure, give me your address. I just bought a car — a convertible!"

Marilyn sensed my excitement. 'Well, hell, let's go to Bob's Big Boy for lunch and eat in the car with the top down."

"Are you serious?"

Her voice and mood changed. "Honestly, Rory, it doesn't matter about the photos or anything else right now. Cukor kicked me off his movie Tuesday. I haven't been a good girl lately. I'm so confused…"

Marilyn's words trailed off. I jotted down her address and directions. I grabbed my coat and tore out of the newsroom just before one o'clock. Somehow, everyday responsibilities that seemed so important a few minutes ago didn't exist. I heard the desperation in her voice. I headed for my car, top down, and pulled onto the street, tires screeching.

It wasn't easy to find her house.

The area surrounding Brentwood was a maze of rural-like streets that wind in and out of small canyons. It didn't feel like the middle of Los Angeles as I made my way through clusters of hidden retreats.

Her house was kind of a rustic, Mexican casa: very run down in a lived-in sort-of-way. The driveway was gravel. Stones crunched by the tires announced my arrival. There were no other cars around. I got out and turned to find Marilyn standing in the doorway, dressed in blue jeans and a white, dress shirt, more like a man's than a woman's, partially tucked in.

As I approached her, she looked haggard. There were lines on her face that weren't there Monday night. I stuck out my hand to shake hers. She reached up and kissed me on the cheek, motioning me to step inside.

She shuffled around the floor of the front room as if she weren't familiar with it, picking up objects here and there, examining them briefly. When she finally said something, she tried to keep it light. With her hands stuffed into her jeans pockets, she looked like a teenager whose parents had just gifted her with a new pet. "This is all mine: my first, real home. What do you think?"

It wasn't what I'd imagined.

I'm like every other movie-star fan. I expected massive opulence with everything in leather with gold trim. Instead, the living room was furnished with a few unmatched chairs scattered around the pink-tiled floor. A brown, rawhide couch that had seen better days faced a brick fireplace. Most of the bricks were blackened from decades of fires. In front of the couch was a coffee table with a glass top, marked with moisture rings from glasses, bottles, and cups.

Somewhat out of place in this room was a spotless, white, baby grand piano placed near the French doors that led to a garden and a swimming pool. I wandered over to the piano and pecked at the keys.

Marilyn's hands were wrapped around a cup of coffee. "Do you play?"

I stopped. "Not at all. It's just impossible for me to be near a piano without poking at the keys."

As she sipped her coffee, I asked her. "Do you play?

She sat at the piano, took a deep breath, and closed her eyes. Her fingers hovered over the keyboard. With some hesitation, she began to play, timidly at first, then with confidence. It sounded like something by J.S. Bach. Then I recognized it: 'Jesu, Joy of man's desiring". She stopped after a few measures and swiveled on the piano bench to face me.

"When I was Norma Jean, I wanted desperately to be a musician. My mother dropped me off at the Hollygrove home for orphans when I was eight. She had another life, and the orphanage kind of acted like a hostel also. I cleaned toilets for my keep, and washed dishes. There was a man who came round every week to give us music lessons. He always wore a smile no matter how badly anyone played. The only thing that kept me alive at that time was my piano lesson once a-week with Mr. Townsend. My life was a living hell." She finished her coffee and sat, staring off.

I didn't know what to say. What was she doing in an orphanage? Where was her mother? I hesitated to break her trance and ask questions. I didn't have to. She volunteered the information as if she were reading my mind.

"The Hollygrove orphanage is located near Vine and El Centro Streets. It's been there since eighteen eighty-eight. I pass by it every so often. I can't get it out of my mind—I mean, the time I spent there."

There was a liquor cabinet next to the piano. She took out a bottle of gin and poured two shots. Without asking me if I wanted one, she handed it to me as if it were a foregone conclusion. She toasted me, mid-air, then kicked-back the gin. "Do you know how I became an actress?"

I took a sip and shook my head.

She poured herself another. "Well, I left the orphanage when I was nine and went back with mother. When I was twelve or thirteen, I looked older than my years. I caught onto men and what they were after at an early age. I married a sailor when I was sixteen."

Here I was, sitting in the front room, sharing a shot of gin with the most famous and elusive of current film stars while she casually revealed her life to me as if I were a close friend. I couldn't believe it.

She paused to twirl the ice cubes in her glass, listening to the sound. She became melancholic.

"That first marriage was not fated to last." She looked up at me with a wistful smile. "I guess none of them were." She took another shot and continued."

"When we split up, I started to do some modeling, and photographers asked me to do some nude shots. I thought, why not? The money was good, and what the hell, once you've seen one nude, you've seen them all, right?"

Marilyn toasted me midair again, this time solo, with her laugh that sounded more like a cry for help.

Her disheveled home echoed her place in the universe today.

Within the confines of these walls, she was different than the person the public knew and worshipped. She was not the larger-than-life image projected on a screen in a dark movie theatre. She wasn't the woman whom I'd met at the Polo Lounge or who came to my apartment.

Devoid of makeup and lacking the energy that propped up her sexy, glamorous persona, Marilyn was just another troubled woman in her mid-thirties having a tough time dealing with life. This reality struck me deeply when I realized that, away from her status as a mega-star, she could have just have been any middle-class housewife from the San Fernando Valley whose life was adrift.

She picked up the bottle of gin, thought twice, and placed it back in the cabinet. "You see, I never forgot about Hollygrove. The six months I spent there have followed me all of my life." She took a cigarette, offered me one, and lit both. The sharp snap of the match striking the box echoed in the tiled living room.

"Besides the piano lessons, there was a small, independent actor's workshop just across the street: The Circle Theatre on El Centro. It's a small playhouse in the round—the closest thing in Hollywood to a legit New York venue.

"In my mid-twenties, I was studying with a well-known Hollywood drama coach. She was friends with the theater's owner, George Boroff.

One day, he told her that Charlie Chaplin was coming to the theater for a kind of master class. Chaplin had insisted on a closed session with no guests. But George snuck us in so that we could watch.

I never forgot George Boroff because of his kindness. He was a real theater person. He directed, wrote, and promoted new playwrights in L.A. His knowing smile was always there, just like the piano teacher at Hollygrove." Marilyn sat with her arms on her legs, leaning over toward me as if she were about to divulge a secret.

"The thing was that my coach had been around the business for a number of years and had quite an ego. I was thrilled to stay in the shadows and watch Chaplin work his magic. At the time, it was the highlight in my life. But the spell was broken when my coach charged the stage challenging Chaplin's comments in front of everyone. I was so embarrassed I left without her, and guess what?"

I shrugged my shoulders.

"The next day, while auditioning for a part in a movie, I met Lee Strasberg. He singled me out and invited me to come to New York to study at his Actor's Studio. So, you see, in a sense, the Circle Theatre launched my career. If I hadn't found out what a jerk my drama coach was, I would have stayed and never gone with Lee." Her eyes grew wide. She slapped me on the knee.

"That's fate in action, buster!" She became energized. "Years later, I took a group of children from Hollygrove to the theater for an excursion. They loved it, and George was so sweet to the kids."

It was going on three o'clock. I was starving. I needed to write down what she was saying. Impossible. I didn't have my briefcase with me. I tried to catalogue her thoughts in my mind to remember them.

Marilyn noticed I was distracted. "What's the matter, Rory, bored?" She stretched her arms above her head. Her nipples nearly punched through her shirt. She wasn't wearing a bra. I began to bulge in my pants. I stood up quickly. "Hardly. I'm just starving."

Marilyn changed directions. "Hey, you promised me a ride in your new convertible. Let's go to Bob's Big Boy on Van Nuys Boulevard, where those cute girls on roller skates bring your food to the car. I'm dying for a hamburger and a vanilla Coke."

She ran over to a closet, fished out a sweater and a scarf, grabbed her huge sunglasses, held out her hand to me, and dragged me to my car.

I couldn't believe this.

One hour later, we were sitting on the lot at Bob's munching on burgers and fries. Other diners in adjoining cars were looking over at us. Rather than trying to avoid their stares, which would attract curiosity, Marilyn just smiled and waved. In a few minutes, the onlookers faded. After all, it couldn't be her; she would never eat at Bob's Big Boy.

Once again, I could kick myself for not having a camera.

At five p.m. I got out of the car to put the top up. It was turning cold in the late afternoon, and Marilyn was chilly. I turned over the two-hundred-and-eighty-three horsepower Chevy V-8 as the waitress rolled away with our trays and my cash. Marilyn became pensive as if she were alone. I didn't feel like prying. I drove her back in silence.

When I pulled into the driveway, there were three people standing by the front door. They saw her and rushed to the car. I panicked. It scared the hell out me.

A middle-aged woman in a business suit came bounding over to the passenger door along with two men ready to drag Marilyn out as if I had kidnapped her. Everyone was yelling. Marilyn gave me a frustrated look and leapt out of the car waving her arms in the air.

"I'm okay...I'm okay, this is a friend of mine. We went out for a bite to eat. Everyone stop it right now. Just stop it!"

She motioned me to join her. "This is Rory Long, a journalist for the *Herald Examiner*. He's working with me on an article that I have sanctioned. He's the man who wrote the wonderful review of Carl's poetry." She turned to smile, motioning me forward. "Rory, this is Evelyn Welmen, my personal assistant."

The woman looked me up and down. "I believe we spoke the other morning on the phone."

I nodded.

Marilyn pointed to the elder of the two men. "Rory, this is my attorney, Max Gingold."

The man offered a courtroom smile and stepped forward to shake my hand. His hand felt clammy. "It's a pleasure to meet you, young man."

I didn't think he could back up that statement with any evidence.

Marilyn smiled genuinely. "And last but not least, this is my press secretary, Jim Donahue."

I couldn't tell how she felt about Welmen or Gingold, but it was obvious that she had a good opinion of Donahue.

He offered a warm handshake. "Nice to meet you, kid. Your boss and I have had many a good argument over his addition at the end of a round of golf."

He seemed genuine.

Donahue looked me straight in the eyes. "I'm happy that the lady is so charged up by this interview project." He handed me his business card. "Call me when you've got something on paper. I'd like to see it." He rolled his eyes. "After all, I'm her press secretary, and believe me, that's not an easy job." He winked.

Marilyn told the trio to go inside and that she'd be right there. Donahue headed for the front door immediately, while Welmen and Gingold hesitated. Marilyn gave them a look, and they followed.

She took my hands in hers. "Rory, I want to thank you for being there for me today. You have no idea what it meant. I have a feeling the rest of this day is not going to be very pleasant. It's all my fault and I know it. So, the memory of that vanilla coke and a Bob's Big Boy with fries will keep me going." She led me around to the driver's door. "Geez, it was just like being in high school. I never got to do that, but I'll bet that's just what it was like!"

I couldn't believe how happy she was. I was sure that her evening with an attorney, press secretary, and the wicked witch of the west would focus on damage control after being booted off Cukor's movie.

I didn't say anything. I had a feeling that this day, spent around the woman who was living inside of the image of Marilyn Monroe, was to be my last. She would drift away into her world, and I would sink into mine.

I had enough material to present her to the public as anything but a joke. She was, by far, the most human of our species, subject to the strengths and weaknesses of existence yet gifted with the power to change the lives of others who merely paid the price of admission and sat in a dark theater watching her move and speak—interacting within the fantasy world known as motion pictures.

A certain sadness came over me as I crept onto the Hollywood Freeway heading south toward the Silver Lake Boulevard exit. I felt that my world would be incomplete without her, and yet, at the same time, I knew I had been privileged enough to spend three days with her: three of the most life-changing days that I had experienced in my young life.

I turned left on Sunset Boulevard off Silver Lake. There was a new billboard at the stoplight: a giant picture of Marilyn with a Coca-Cola in her hands, wearing a low-cut, pink sweater with slacks to match, and that smile, that face, that look that only she had ever been capable of projecting.

I pulled into my garage, shut off the engine, and sat wondering: where do I go from here? How do I begin to handle the rest of my life? Will I be stupid enough to judge all other women by her?

I slipped the key into my front door and started to laugh. Okay, Rory, back to business. Get off your ass and write a series of articles on the most publicly recognized woman no one truly knows.

# Chapter 18

Another restless night.

What was she to do? Her life was a mess. A year and a half had passed since her last film. This week, Cukor fired her. The fact Gable passed away soon after finishing *The Misfits* still haunted. She often woke up in the middle of the night and saw his face suspended in mid-air—that smile coming straight toward her: a severe reminder of the futility of life.

Two pink pills went down smoothly with a glass of wine. The tiny mother's helpers kicked in quickly with the aid of alcohol. She felt like writing.

She crawled into bed with her pen and journal, but the items became buried in the comforter and satin sheets. She patted around for them but gave up. On her bedside table were all of her journals. There were nine of them, dating from nineteen-fifty to nineteen fifty-eight. They looked strange, as if they didn't belong to her. In fact, after reading Plato, she wondered if any of our thoughts belonged to us.

Plato believed that everything we thought and imagined gathered into the Milky Way, just like C.G. Jung's *Collective Consciousness* or the *anima mundi* of the Neo-Platonists. Marilyn liked the concept that all of our ideas, good and bad, were deposited at a place in the universe, and that, if we had a good antenna, we could access these great ideas—they would just come to us.

She stretched her legs and arms and her pen and journal resurfaced. She began to make a diary entry but was overtaken by a poem. It just poured out.

The silence
Fills my head with unbearable sounds.
Pitch blackness comes

with monsters lurking
in the shadows.
My blood aches,
changes direction
while the world sleeps.
I find peace-even in threatening shadows.

She was never sure what she'd written until it was finished. Each time she read something new, it was as if someone else had created it. All of her poems seemed to be composed by another hand that worked like hers but was not. The words seemed to undulate on the paper like a bed of snakes in the swamp. The poem mirror-imaged her feelings.

Right now, she felt she'd lost everything that she had worked so hard for. Was it all her fault? She was always under pressure. All day, every day, only the nights were hers, except they never truly were: she shared them with her nightmares.

She shuffled through her journals and picked out one marked, "1950." In her stoned, floating mood, thumbing through the pages, she tried to find a thought written down then that would reflect how she felt now.

It wasn't to be. A fog hovered over her bed. The pills were at their peak. Marilyn felt weightless, ageless, and unhooked from the gravitational pull of the moon and stars. Each word she read conjured up an image before her eyes: a symbol of her longing—passions and misgivings.

She turned to another page. She wrote with a quivering hand.

Alone, I am always alone!!

Yes, that was the problem then, and in the past years it hadn't changed. She had been so strong yet at times so weak that it seemed logical to end it all just for the sake of peace and quiet, of not existing. What was the purpose of life on this planet, moving around with billions of others who can't make sense of it?

The image of a watercolor by William Blake filled her imagination. It was an ocean, and in the ocean was a dolphin, and on its back was a man. The painting reflected the neo-platonic belief that when you met with death, you would travel on the back of a dolphin, reviewing your entire life from the very last thing you experienced all the way back to the womb. Then, you'd be released from the bondage of matter: the body, the sepulcher that breathes.

In her self-induced haziness, she realized one journal was missing: the one that Rory found after their interview. That journal was her favorite. It had most of her thoughts about history and the arts.

Rory. He was different.

She believed in him. Having only read the article he wrote on Carl, she could see his future. Spending the time with him put her completely at ease. The night she slept on his couch, she enjoyed one of the best nights of sleep she'd had in months.

He was so young. She had always needed an older man beside her—the security of a father figure, which she had been deprived of as a child. Rory was nearly fifteen years her junior. When they first talked on the phone, he'd called her *ma'am*. That affected her in a strange way. At that moment, she contemplated growing old: traveling down a road until you disappear.

As stoned as she was, she managed to fish up the newspaper from the floor to reread his article on the Black Dahlia in this morning's *Examiner*. It tugged at her memory.

Marilyn put a stack of pillows behind her to support her back. She took a bottle of nearly empty cognac and poured a shot.

Elizabeth Short.

Marilyn would never forget the two days when their paths crossed that summer before the girl's grizzly murder.

She'd just filmed her first role with dialogue. It was the Marx Brothers' last movie, *Go West*.

Groucho surprised her. He could talk for hours about literature and history, punning jokes amidst an accurate discourse on wars and man's basic inhumanity to man.

On the other hand, Chico was no surprise. True to form, he spent all his time trying to bed her down.

Her fondest memories were the moments shared with Harpo. He was wise beyond his years. He told stories about musicians and composers that were a scream. He was mischievous, like a fairy in Shakespeare. He was observant, always having a kind word handy for those who needed one.

After the last day of shooting, Marilyn decided to visit Hollygrove. Returning to the hellhole of her youth would be like a consecration or an initiation: an ablution to cleanse her soul.

She spotted Liz when she walked in. The girl turned toward Marilyn with that look of, *I know you, don't I?*

Marilyn saw herself in the newly-arrived, twenty-four-year-old Hollywood hopeful who would wait tables, as those who came before her, hoping to be discovered.

The up-and-coming star felt sorry for her. She was all alone and so hopeful. Marilyn knew firsthand the rejection the girl would experience.

She invited Liz Short to lunch.

The two sat and chatted at Patti's Cafe on Santa Monica Boulevard for nearly two hours. Marilyn told her all about her time at Hollygrove. Liz was only staying there for two nights. She had managed to find a cold-water flat on Franklin Avenue that she could afford at least for a month or two to see if she could get a break into pictures.

They talked about men.

Marilyn had already been through the Hollywood ringer: that unmarked, open field laced with predators at every corner. Liz Short hailed from a small town. Marilyn listened attentively to her dreams, hopes, and desire to succeed, knowing what she would be going through during her introduction to Hollywood's dark side.

However, it was their second encounter that put Marilyn on edge.

They met again by accident in the Max Factor cosmetic shop on Hollywood Boulevard. Liz told her about a Hollywood division detective whose father was a prominent doctor in the community: a surgeon, a specialist.

She had just been hired as a waitress at a café on Melrose Avenue, close to the Hollywood precinct. The lawman had singled her out while having lunch. A few days later, he showed up with his father. The mature doctor was attracted to the young girl. He arrived several days in a row for lunch, finally asking her out for dinner.

Liz confessed to Marilyn that she wasn't sure what to do, but being that his son was a cop, and the man was a doctor, she accepted the offer.

Marilyn shivered as the girl told her of the macabre sexual acts the man wanted to explore for a sizeable fee.

Liz cut and ran.

Not long after, her brutal murder made headlines. Marilyn recoiled in horror at the news. When she read the article and discovered that the body had been hacked into two pieces and all of the blood had been drained off, the first thing she thought about was the doctor. Liz had told her his name.

When Rory mentioned he was working on a piece for the paper about the Dahlia, Marilyn hesitated to tell him what she knew.

She felt guilty.

They hadn't spoken in several days. He told her that he would phone when he had the first article of her interview ready for her approval. That was last week. She would wait until tomorrow and then call him at the paper, or maybe at home.

The one woman in the world who could have any man groveling at her feet found her thoughts drifting to the young, lanky journalist with the understanding heart. She flashed back on her night spent at his apartment.

She never told him that, during the night, she got up for some water and snuck into his bedroom to watch him sleep. He looked like an angel, a cherubim who had come down from the clouds.

Hollywood, in its usual, inexplicable fashion, would present the depressed star with an unexpected carrot on the end of a stick. One more chance would be in the offing.

# Chapter 19

My insomnia was starting to fade since I began the habit of walking around the neighborhood before going to bed. I was just taking off my coat when the phone rang. It was eleven forty-five. I knew who it was before I picked up the receiver.

"Rory, I'm sorry to bother you."

I pulled myself out of sleep-ready mode. "Marilyn, I'm so glad you called. Actually, I didn't want to bother you, but I'm nearly finished with our piece and I wanted to get a copy for you to look over. You see, it's turned into more than an interview article; it's become part of…" I was nervous as hell and could have gone on forever. Fortunately, she picked up on my youthful enthusiasm and cut in.

"That's wonderful, Rory. I can't wait to read what you've done. Listen, I have some great news. I'm having a meeting with the studio heads in the morning. Cukor wants me back on the set. I'm spending the night in a trailer on the lot, that way there is no way for me to be late or not show up." She was excited.

Word of mouth had it that since the director let her go, the studio heads figured out that no matter how erratic she was, they desperately needed her to finish the film. She was in most of the shots. It would be impossible to replace her without shooting the production from the beginning, and that wasn't on the table. There was already a bundle of bucks tied up in this project. They convinced the veteran director to give her a second chance.

"Well, what would you like me to do? I can come by the lot tomorrow and drop off my manuscript?"

A few seconds of silence. "Rory, I'm scared. I'm afraid if I spend the night alone, I'll feel insecure in the morning. You would do me a big favor if you could come by tonight. I need the company. No, I need *your* company."

I was too shocked to respond immediately.

She cracked. "You can sleep on my couch in the trailer. What the hell, I slept on yours!"

I tried to come up with an answer as fast as I could. Weisman will probably have me shot if he finds out that I spent another night with the Goddess, especially after the arrival of the photos. But, did I really give a shit?

No. The bottom line: I wanted to be there for her—and with her.

"Give me some directions. I'll come as soon as I can."

Marilyn was gleeful.

I was learning that hero worship was highly overrated. People are attracted to one another by serendipitous circumstances, or they aren't. It's as simple as that.

Never in my life could I have predicted that one day I would call Marilyn Monroe a friend, and here I was, heading out in the dead of night because she called and said she needed me. Besides, I wanted to see how comfortable her couch was.

I'd never been on a movie lot. I expected, like most, that the place would ooze a bigger-than-life atmosphere, which sparked those glamorous, romantic visions about Hollywood. The truth was, in the dead of night, as I began to search for trailer twenty-nine, I felt as though I were walking through an airplane or appliance factory. Everything seemed mechanical, robotic, and void of human touch: steel cranes and beams, railroad tracks running down alleys with carts full of hand tools, heavy power drills and saws. It was quiet and dark. I thought I was in the middle of nowhere instead of in the heart of Hollywood.

Her voice came from behind me.

"Over here, Rory."

Marilyn was perched on the steps of an Airstream trailer, backlit by the light coming from inside. She was wearing a silk robe with nothing underneath. The illumination silhouetted her figure. I walked toward her with a lump in my throat. Was this a smart thing to be doing? After all, the issue of the photos had not been resolved. What the hell, I was here now.

The plaque above the trailer door was a wooden star painted silver. Below was a slide-in-slide-out nameplate. Greer Garson's name was displayed, obviously to keep the curious away from Marilyn.

The trailer was roomier inside than I'd imagined: more cozy than cramped. Two small lamps at either end provided dim light. Marilyn didn't offer me a hug, a kiss, or even a handshake. She climbed onto a small stool near the closest lamp in her white-satin robe with her legs crossed, exposed to her thigh. She began to file her fingernails, eyeing the results.

I sat at a small booth near the mini-kitchen. She seemed distant. I couldn't tell if she were sober or stoned. Silence reined, not a word was spoken. She acted as if she were alone. I'd begun to think that my choice to be with her was a mistake. It seemed she'd forgotten her invitation.

I took out the manuscript. I desperately wanted to explain to her that, while working on it, our time together had woven itself into the structure, that it was impossible to separate the two. I felt caught up in the mystery that was her.

She looked up. "Is that it?"

She held out her hands, and I passed it to her. She turned it over and over, feeling the weight. The manuscript was nearly one hundred typed pages and I wasn't close to finishing it. She passed it back.

"Rory, I can't read about myself. It's too weird. Would you read it to me? Would you like a drink?"

Before I could answer either question, she got off the stool and bent over a cabinet, retrieving two shot glasses and a bottle of Irish whisky. The silk robe lined the crevice of her buttocks. She poured us both a shot. We lit a cigarette, saluted each other, and emptied our glasses. The whisky gave off that cool burn all the way down.

She stared off into space and then blinked her eyes several times. "Thank you for being here, Rory. I know I'm acting strange, but you must believe that I'm very happy that you've come by." She poured us each another tumbler. "I'm so nervous about tomorrow. I've got a lot riding on what happens."

She motioned toward the manuscript. "Okay, Mr. Long, tell me all about myself." She sat at the other end of the banquette, closed her eyes, and laid her head on her arms on the table.

I scanned the first page quickly and dove in.

Beyond Stardom: interviews with Marilyn Monroe
By Rory Daniel Long
Preface to the reader

*The task of any journalist is to accurately depict the circumstances surrounding their chosen subject. In this case, the private thoughts of a public figure worshipped by millions of adoring fans.*

*A series of one-on-one interviews is the basis of this work. I could not imagine a more difficult task than to attempt to explain to the public about the number one, box-office film star's life lived away from the big screen: her guarded intellectual pursuits. Marilyn Monroe began her search for self-knowledge early in life. This is verified by the extensive journals she's kept for over a decade, filled with original poems, essays, and historical timelines—reflections about history, ancient and modern.*

*It is my hope that you will be as inspired by her journey as I was. Marilyn Monroe is a thinker who continues to reflect upon the eternal questions: who are we? Why are we here? Where are we going?*

I paused to observe her reaction. She was sound asleep and snoring lightly. I closed the cover and had a smoke. That was my first critical response. Maybe I'm not as hot as I think I am. It was two a.m. A small leather couch on the other side of the trailer beckoned to me. I snapped off the lamps, moved onto the couch, and fell into a deep slumber.

The heavy scent of Chanel No. 5 woke me. My eyes shot open. Marilyn stood over me with an unforgettable smile. It took me a few seconds to focus. Right, I'm in a trailer, on a movie lot in Hollywood, and I've just spent another night sleeping in the company of the Goddess.

I rubbed my eyes. "What time is it?"

She stroked my brow. "It's time for you to go so I can get ready for the meeting."

The aroma of fresh coffee drifted through the trailer. I gave Marilyn that poor-puppy-dog look.

She slapped my shoulder. "Men, you're all alike!"

I wasn't awake enough to react.

She kneeled down next to me. "I'm sorry, Rory. I didn't mean that, especially to you. You're not like most men. Not at all."

If I could get her to write that down and sign it, I would be home free with women for the rest of my life.

I looked at my watch: six thirty a.m. "Okay, I'm on my way." I sipped my coffee while getting dressed and noticed my manuscript was on the small dining table, opened up to the midway point. An ashtray with three butts in it and the half-empty bottle of whisky was nearby.

Marilyn sat down and continued to read. "This is very good, Rory. You'll need to get a copy to Jim Donahue, okay? Also, you'll need to meet with Gingold. He'll have legal papers for us to sign."

I nodded my head while buttoning my shirt. "Whatever you say, my dear." Still in a stupor, I caught myself right after those words tumbled out. The most endearing look came over the star's face.

She rose from the table and gave me kiss on the cheek. "That's one of the sweetest things a man has ever said to me. A very common phrase, but delivered in a very uncommon way." Her eyes fixed on mine for a few moments. "You'd better go now. The early birds will be arriving soon to begin another day of hammering, drilling and, painting to make make-believe seem real."

I drove home down Sunset Boulevard a few minutes before seven a.m. to get ready for work.

"...*To make make-believe seem real.*"

# Chapter 20

Long before Hollywood could boast of being the center of the movie-making universe, there was Glendale, Echo Park, and Silver Lake. Silent filmmakers Mack Sennett and Charlie Chaplin used these locations when their careers began.

Standing at the apex of Silver Lake and Glendale Boulevards is an unpretentious, local watering hole called the *Mixer*. The bar was built by silent film cowboy legend, Tom Mix. The cowboy movie star wanted a place where he and his crew could kick up their heels after a day's shoot in the hot sun.

The prim woman in her early sixties had a rendezvous with her contact at this out-of-the-way location. She sat uneasily in the dark observing the customers at three o'clock that afternoon. Some of the women had that look of being in a drunken stupor, as depicted by Renoir in his paintings a century ago. The men smiled the smile conjured by too many drinks.

Evelyn Welmen tried to calm down by taking in the atmosphere of pure movie cowboy. There were black-and-white photos of the great man himself, alongside other icons of the Hollywood western: Bob Steel, Lash La Rue, Gene Autry, Roy Rogers, Hoot Gibson as well as dozens of photos of horses fully decorated in hand-tooled leather saddles awash with sterling-silver buckles. Guns in holsters were set in display cases, and spurs, chaps, and a pile of Stetson cowboy hats were piled on a table in the corner.

Sipping a glass of ice water, the recovering alcoholic mused over her first day on the job with the star. She'd received a phone call from a person claiming to be affiliated with a government organization of fact gatherers. The man recounted her past history during the McCarthy era, and said, in no uncertain terms, that since she would be in close contact with Monroe, it would be required of her to keep a record of Marilyn's social life. If she followed orders, she would be able to wake up every morning until her natural life ran its course. However, lack of cooperation would lead to an early dismissal from her place in the sun. She didn't need any help interpreting this threat.

After this contact, she cautiously asked for information within her circle regarding the anonymous caller: what organization might they be linked to? Usually, reliable sources who maintained political ties got back to her saying it would be best to ask no questions.

She had no choice. This invisible society appeared to be a coalition of persons who took their calling in life seriously. What this *calling* amounted to was a mystery even to those who were aware of their existence. She was nervous. She had the right to be. Her meeting with a member of the *group* had no guarantees for her safety.

The interior of the Mixer, like most bars, was dimly lit. Whenever the front door opened, a streak of daylight shot across the sawdust covered floor, creating a silhouette of the patrons coming and going.

Evelyn watched as the door swung open and the bulky figure of a man entered, heading straight for her booth. He sat without a greeting, his eyes focused straight ahead as if she weren't there. "Do you have the information?"

Evelyn nodded, handing him an envelope.

The man perused the contents while continuing. "Does she know about the photos yet?"

Evelyn's voice was shrill and unsure. "I don't know…she hasn't mentioned it to me, and I think she would if she knew about them."

The contact talked to Evelyn without looking at her. "Has she seen Rory Long since that night?"

"Yes. They were together at her home a few days later."

As a waitress approached the couple, the man waved her away. "Well then, I think we can assume that she knows about the photos if she and Long have been together since they were sent to the paper." Finally, he looked at Evelyn with an expression that caused a cold shiver to run through her body.

"I'm afraid you will have to do more to stay on top of the situation. Am I clear?"

Evelyn nodded.

The man stood and tossed a ten-dollar bill on the table. "I'll be in touch. Keep at it."

He was gone in seconds.

This was her first encounter with a member of the *group*. She prayed it would be the last.

Although a recovering alcoholic, Evelyn ordered a vodka Collins with a twist. She needed a drink like never before.

# Chapter 21

The seven figures were seated around a conference table in an obscure wing of a Federal building in Washington D.C. They were in a heated debate. Their inside contact had done her job, but her efforts had not yielded what they'd hoped for.

Since their inception, it had been the policy of this organization to keep an eye on certain persons in the public eye who had close relationships with high-profile leaders in government. The mission of this covert group: to protect the good names of elected officials in power to insure a path to global unification under the leadership of the United States government, as the founding fathers of our great nation intended.

The Governing Regents of Universal Principles, aka "The GROUP," had been in existence for decades no matter which party was in power. Selection for membership in this elite, covert organization was stringent, requiring potential members to undergo extreme background checks as well as the willingness to take a pledge to die for the cause. Their manipulations take place off the grid: they answer only to their agenda and themselves.

Two women and five men currently make up the membership. One of the women pounded a gavel on the massive tabletop. It sounded a like a bomb exploding. Madam X was the current chairman of the society. She demanded order.

"This is pure nonsense. We are debating a decided issue. We all know what has to be done. We will never be able to count on this individual to keep her lips sealed. If and when she decides to disclose the information regarding one of our past members and his indiscretion, it could lead to destroying years of planning and accomplishments.

"It is ironic that the editor of the *Herald* opened a can of worms when he gave Huey Long's grandson the Dahlia assignment. The kid is smart. Even though we convinced our counterpart at the Bureau to have Weisman take him off the case, Mr. Long may choose to continue the investigation on his own." The chairwoman paused to light a small cigar. Others joined her with pipes and cigarettes.

"All we really need to do is set the date somewhere in the first week of August and handpick a team to carry out the mission. It must look like an accident."

She turned to address one of the members. "Speaking of accidents, can you explain to those present what was on your mind when you took those photos?"

The man's shirt was soaked with sweat. He knew this was coming.

"I thought we could use them at some point to convince the individual to remain silent. It would offer us an alternative plan. I didn't think that it would cause such a mess. It's just that, after I agreed to go along with the decision to eliminate the individual, my conscience began to eat away at me."

The chairwoman listened while finishing her cigar, tossing it into a large, marble ashtray in the center of the table. She cast an intense expression. "Key phrase here...*I didn't think.*" She leaned back in her chair folding her hands across her chest. "Knowing our rules and regulations, why on earth did you go outside the organization with a rogue alternative?"

The man, who felt on trial, shook his head and shrugged his shoulders, silently signaling his inability to defend himself.

His inner thoughts told him there was nothing he could do. The fact that the group was willing to assassinate a popular, public personality on the pretext that she might divulge information linking one or their past members to the Black Dahlia murder was unthinkable. It was taking things too far. He'd gone along with the vote, but since that time, he'd regretted his decision and made his alternative plan in desperation.

Other members of the *group* were whispering to one another. The heat of their collective thoughts seared through him. He knew, once he'd agreed to join the organization, his membership was for life: that period of time to be adjusted according to performance.

The chairwoman continued. "Weren't you aware of the risk you were taking which might put the organization in jeopardy?" She paused for effect. "What if the person doing the delivery was recognized by the person signing for the parcel?" Her expression grew darker. "At the least, whoever received the package might be able to recall a nametag on a uniform, which would make it easy to trace the item back to the source." The chairwoman pulled another cigar out of her purse but set it on the table. "Your decision to act independently, even though you believed you were working in favor of the *group*, may have cost us our existence. I consider it pure luck that it hasn't thus far."

She turned to the panel as a simultaneous murmur filled the room. "That is why it is imperative that we act quickly."

One of the other male members spoke up. "I've cast a horoscope for the ideal date. Mars is in conjunction with Venus on the fifth of August."

"Then that's it. We know from the past to trust your astrological calculations, your eminence."

The chairwoman looked around the table for confirmation. She returned her focus to the guilty party. Her intense gaze returned.

"I'm afraid you've stepped over the line on this one. You've known, since your initiation, that every move within our circle is made in unison. It is the total cooperation of this society that has kept us strong throughout the years. There is, and has never been, any room in this body for acting on one's own authority without the consent and blessing of the entire membership."

Tension filled the chamber as the man felt a silent judgment was passed. The woman leaned forward, resting her elbows on the massive table. "I'm afraid we will have to ask you for your resignation."

He froze. He knew his days were numbered. He'd been a member for five years and had witnessed the dismissal of another member. That man died of a heart attack within forty-eight hours.

The six remaining members stood. The guilty party rose to his feet searching for a sympathetic expression, but none could be found.

Gathering up his things, he looked back for the last time at the invisible consortium whose net was cast across the globe.

If he were lucky, he could book an airline ticket out of the country in the next few hours and buy himself some time. But he knew that the minute he walked through that door, the odds were against him of even making it to the airport.

# Chapter 22

The Blarney Castle, located on Vermont Avenue, typified Hollywood. A theme restaurant/bar, complete with Scottish plaid wall hangings, bagpipes, suits of armor, and mediaeval swords crossed in pairs with hammered shields as backdrops. It was a real slice of Hollywood, just as phony as a film director's beret. The only items on the premises from Scotland were a few bottles of imported malt whisky. Most of the décor was purchased from prop companies along Melrose Avenue.

Weisman and Donahue topped off their lunch with a second martini. Another week was coming to a close.

"I really shouldn't." The press agent said in a half-jocular way.

"Right!" Weisman answered without really listening. He was contemplating the redheaded waitress with the overstuffed bosom as he slipped her a twenty-dollar bill. "Keep the change, darling," Weisman said with a wink. She giggled as she moved on.

Weisman turned to Jim. "Your only responsibility in the immediate future, my good friend, is to meet Syd and me tomorrow at Griffith Park so you can watch me beat the pants off of that yokel." Weisman winked at his friend. The two men saluted each other and downed most of their second cocktail.

Donahue wiped his lips with the back of his hand. "You really are one incorrigible son-of-a-bitch, Al, you always have been."

Weisman sucked his olive off the toothpick. "That's part of my indefatigable charm, Jim…along with my sprightly wit and unmatched sense of humor."

Jim Donahue was an unlikely call to be a press agent. He never met the basic requirement that was the mandatory screaming and yelling above the crowd. Jim was quiet and somewhat reclusive. His P.T. Barnum side was conjured out of hiding when required to make sure that his employer, in this case Monroe, had her name plastered all over newspapers, magazines, radio, and now television.

His second obligation to the star was to keep her name out of the mud when possible. Jim ran defense for Marilyn when malicious rumors were spread. He kept her fans informed of her projects. Jim was her direct line to the public. He was privy to a fair share of secrets about the blonde's private life that had nothing to do with sex, money, or drugs, along with being her father confessor.

He knew her past as well as her present. It was his job to insure her future.

The star's career was on hold. Marilyn's future was one reason for calling his friend to have a bite. He needed to talk about the relationship between his boss, Marilyn, and Weisman's employee, Rory. Jim had been a major player in getting the heads of *Twentieth* and Cukor on the same page about rehiring the star. He wanted to make sure nothing got in the way of Marilyn's return.

One of Weisman's skills, which had kept him at the top of the heap, was his capacity to be one step ahead of whomever he was dealing with. Tucked away in Weisman's coat pocket were the photos.

After the two men topped off their second martini, Weisman opened Pandora's box. "Okay, Jim. Let's cut the crap. You didn't invite me here today to see who could be the first to crawl to their car after a few martinis."

Jim was ready to respond, when Weisman set the photo of the kiss on the table. Jim's jaw fell. Weisman smiled. "I take it that this engaging proof of intimacy between our two friends has not made it across your desk?"

Donahue, still unable to speak, just shook his head back and forth.

Weisman tossed the other photos on the table. "Well then, I can scratch another suspect off my list."

The press agent was aghast. "What in the hell...who in the hell...where in the hell did these come from?"

Weisman looked around the room and then lowered his voice. "That is the question of the hour. These photos, and several more, were waiting for me in an envelope two weeks ago when I arrived at work. Since then, I've determined that Hoover and his gang had nothing to do with them, and as far as I can tell, no one has produced these snapshots for any other news source but the *Herald*." Weisman tried to take a sip, forgetting his glass was empty. "At first, I thought it might be one of the gossip mags, but nope. These intimate pictures just seemed to have popped up from nowhere. And it would appear, through this photographic evidence, that your boss and my employee have become close friends. It might even be safe to assume that they are on the verge of doing the bouncy-bounce, if they haven't already."

Donahue was glassy-eyed. He wasn't an afternoon drinker. The photos took him for a loop. The picture of Marilyn in an embrace with the cub reporter made him so tense that he was about to have a stroke.

Somehow, Weisman's phrase, "…doing the *bouncy-bounce*," was a trigger that set off an uncontrollable shriek of laughter from both men as they realized how preposterous the last few weeks had been. There wasn't a screenwriter in Hollywood that could come up with this story line.

It started a chain reaction. In a matter of seconds, the crowded bar was howling, not sure of the joke. It didn't matter; it's only the laugh that counts.

# Chapter 23

I didn't know what to do with myself. My time with Marilyn seemed finished. There'd been no contact since the night in the trailer. After her meeting that morning with the big wigs, she left a message for me at the paper.

Three words: *I got it!*

That was two weeks ago. I've really missed her. My ego had swollen to the point that I believed I occasionally crossed her mind. I must. That is my current reason to get up in the morning.

From day one of this adventure, I was aware of the danger.

She was so damn easy to be with. It was like hanging out with one of the guys. She never acted the star when we were together. I became too comfortable, feeling that our time together would continue. The inner voice of my conceit whispered that she cared for me, that she recognized a quality in my nature that others missed.

I was foolish enough to believe that I could offer her something no one had given her before: real, honest and unselfish love.

I took our relationship seriously: that was precocious youth, front and center.

The series of interviews had expanded into a lengthy essay divided into installments. I included observations of my time with Marilyn—somehow that seemed necessary. I turned the project into Weisman days ago. I've heard nothing since.

The inauguration of the series was set to go to print the first week in August.

I was too young and inexperienced to have enough confidence in my skill. And now I was having doubts about adding personal observations about the star into the text. Was it my place to do so? Will Weisman dress me down for that?

In the back of my mind, I began to think about being judged by thousands of readers as they sipped their morning coffee.

I had a long talk with Rose. My mother told me how proud she was, and, of course, she had advice concerning my next move. "You will acquire some kind of instant fame when these articles hit the streets."

She sounded like an attorney.

"The wolves will be out in packs chasing you through the forest. Opportunities will come flying through the front door. Think every offer through calmly. Don't let your ego make decisions." She paused. "Do you have legal counsel?"

I told her that she sounded qualified. We laughed. That was the first light-hearted moment I'd had in days.

I tried to explain that the interviews were important, but forming a bond with Marilyn, regardless of how long it lasts, meant the most to me. Rose listened, saying she understood, but in my heart I don't think anyone could understand.

While writing the articles, I kept another folder full of Marilyn's prose and poems I'd copied out. The possibility of writing a book about our brief time spent together was haunting me. I wasn't sure I should for one reason: people would think I was grandstanding.

In truth, I had to wonder if it wasn't my pumped-up ego that wanted to go public, pounding my chest like Tarzan and screaming down from the heights: "Look at me, I've spent time with Marilyn Monroe, and she even kissed me!" A man can be a complete fool at any age—from nineteen to ninety.

From another viewpoint, to write a book about my time with Marilyn would be considered, in most circles, a chance for career advancement. I had a problem with this. I could never attempt to further my status by exposing intimate moments shared with a public icon.

All I knew for sure was that something inside me needed to write down my time spent with her in detail. I needed to see if it's real. Truth nonsense, nonsense truth: that is the everyday philosophy in a city where the borders of reality are constantly in flux.

Carol Thompson called.

Max Gingold had scheduled a meeting between all parties for Monday afternoon in his Century city office. There were papers to sign concerning the interviews. Too bad we can't copyright life. I relived my moments with her every day.

I no longer take walks around the neighborhood to induce a good nights' sleep. I seldom go to bed before midnight. I have a cigarette and a shot of whisky and curl up on the couch where Marilyn slept.

Tonight, I watched the yellow glow from the street lamp highlight the spines in my bookcase. Something was odd.

I knew all of the titles on the shelves. One looked unfamiliar. I rolled off the couch and pulled it out. It was a slender volume bound in black book cloth with the title on the spine in gold: a first edition of Carl Sandburg's premier book of verse. I opened the cover, and on the flyleaf, a dedication was written—it was from Sandburg.

*All things that matter in life are within reach if you are aware of their presence.*

The one on the inside cover was from Marilyn to me.

*Rory,*

*I shall always wonder how long it took you to find this book in your library. Carl offered it to me years ago. I'm now giving it to you. You are a good friend, and I shall always remember your kindness. Please keep writing. You are gifted.*

*Marilyn, June 7, 1962 Silver Lake*

My ears began to ring.

I became light-headed. I swung my legs off the couch and planted my feet squarely on the floor. I needed grounding. When did she do this? Normally, I go through my library every week. I realized I hadn't looked at a book since I began to write the interviews. I couldn't move. I held the book open to her dedication and reread it several times.

It was definitely a good-bye message. When a person tells you they will *always remember,* that's a sure sign of no further contact. Marilyn must have done this the night she spent on my couch. Did she think, when we met, that we would become friends?

Even if her dedication was an affectionate kiss off, I felt that she was part of my life. It could be that aspect of the human quality that simply cannot let go of emotional peaks even when the chance of fulfilling some fairytale imagery is next to hopeless.

At the same time, another woman plagued me. Along with Marilyn, I had been courting the dead.

My emotional tie to Elizabeth Short would not go away. Her brutal murder had somehow captured my sympathy with a stronger grip than I thought possible.

The fact that J. Edgar had contacted Weisman early on in my investigation, ordering him to take me off the project made me curious. Shortly after the phone call, my first article along with my notes disappeared. Then, they mysteriously reappeared.

At first, when Weisman edited my Dahlia article, I was angry. But soon I realized that fear of possible reprisals from Hoover had prompted him to tone it down. I dropped the charges.

This was more than my overactive mind could cope with. Why would anyone care about what I had to say about the unsolved crime? I remember the look on Marilyn's face when I mentioned my assignment to her. She cringed. I hadn't thought much of it at the time, but now it seemed important.

I took all of my notes on Liz Short's murder and went to bed. I was still convinced that a prominent doctor from Los Angeles was involved.

I fell asleep wanting to talk it over with Marilyn. Something's there, I can feel it. Anyway, I now had an excuse to call.

# Chapter 24

Weisman could feel the years kicking in after Donahue and he decided to have one more martini for the road. Between the stress and the long hours he'd been putting in lately, he was past exhaustion.

He stayed in his office after quitting time to go over Rory's first draft on the interview with Marilyn. Over all, he liked what he read, but something inside him was uneasy.

The kid had done the impossible.

He landed on the moon by merely jumping over a wall. Marilyn Monroe, the most infamous of all females, made contact with Rory his first day on the paper. The next thing we know, they're kissing cousins. This was the problem. You learn very early in this business, that if it's too good to be true, it isn't, or there might be an element of danger around the corner.

The grandson of Huey Long had done himself justice as a journalist.

The conversation between the two was intelligent, as the wide-eyed film star expressed herself in a concise and direct language. Rory's commentary was accessible to all, delivered in a style of spoken prose that had the capacity to entertain as well as enlighten. This project could earn our young prodigy an award—and beyond. That is, if he's still around to receive it.

Weisman could feel dark forces nearby. He was still perplexed about the source of the photos. The fact that no other players on the field received the images made things worse. Why in the hell would anyone do that and then disappear? Unless...

It was ten o'clock. Except for the janitors who would come around eleven, he had the floor to himself. Late-night journalists were out on assignments.

Weisman swiveled around in his chair and burst onto the news floor, stalking every inch of it going from desk to desk and hoping for a miracle. "That's gotta be it." He studied each desk.

When he arrived at Bunny Blanchard's *Woman's Day* cubicle, he paused. The reflected light from neon signs, coming through the high windows shone on her desktop. He thought he spotted the corner of a gold-embossed envelope sticking out from underneath her desk blotter. He pulled it out. The return address was the Beverly Glen Hotel. Without hesitation, he read the note inside.

*My dear B.B. -All is going according to plan. The group has made their decision.*

Weisman's curiosity peaked.

He tore Blanchard's *Woman's Day* desk apart. He went through all the drawers and files that Bunny had kept for years. Actually, he never could stand the bitch. She was always whining about her working conditions, spending most of her time wandering around the news floor looking over everyone's shoulder for a tidbit she could steal and insert in her column that reeked of trivial and unimportant items. He was dying to fire her, but she was popular with homemakers.

Weisman found another note from the same source. It was dated June 15, 1962. He read it holding the first note next to his new find:

*Bunny. I am stuck with these people. There is no way I can get away from the group. What am I to do? The one who loves you most! EW*

For some reason, the initials "EW" rang a bell.

When Rory was preparing for the interview, Weisman had requested that he keep a list of the people encountered during his time with Marilyn. One name on Rory's list had the initials "EW." Could the notes to Bunny be from Marilyn's personal assistant, Evelyn Welmen?

He remembered an article that appeared in the entertainment section of the *Herald* when she was hired by John Huston to work on *The Misfits*. She, just like Weisman, had been attacked by McCarthy and Hoover.

She was also known to be a lesbian, which was played up at the same time she was being accused of communist sympathies. Her sexual preference, becoming public knowledge, forced her into hiding for several years. The woman was now Marilyn's assistant or watchdog or…? He knew that Monroe often booked into the Beverly Glen to get away from it all.

If these notes were from Welmen, did that mean that Blanchard and she were lovers?

Weisman sat at Blanchard's desk. It was ten forty-five. Not a sound could be heard on the streets. He took a blank sheet of paper out of her desk drawer and scrolled it into her typewriter. He made a list:

1. The grandson of Huey Long comes to work at the Herald—
2. Marilyn Monroe falls into his life—She wants Rory to tell the world her big *secret*—
3. I give him the Black Dahlia assignment—
4. Hoover sends two men to my house to warn me about Long—
5. Hoover calls me at home and asks me to take Rory off the BD investigation—
6. Rory's article on the BD and his notes disappear, only to mysteriously reappear a few days late—
7. Marilyn visits Rory—Someone takes pictures of their intimate moments and sends them to me—
8. The big question: why haven't these photos shown up somewhere else?

The senior editor now believed that the mole in the newsroom was Bunny. Was Blanchard and Welmen tied in with an organization that was up to no good? Was someone out to get Marilyn, and possibly Rory?

He reread the two notes from Evelyn to Bunny.

…The group has decided…can't get away from the group…

Weisman tidied up her desk as the janitors were ambling into the newsroom. He grabbed his hat and coat and headed down the dark hallway toward the elevator. There was a sense of being watched. He took the stairway, all six floors, and ran out of the building, screeching the tires as he pulled away, his heart pumping. In a few blocks, he checked his rearview mirror to see if he was being followed. No sign of another car on his tail.

He felt safe, for now.

He drove home down Wilshire. He was thinking clearly again. Who is this *group*? Did they take the photos and then, for some reason, stop distribution?

Was that the mistake Welmen referred to in one of her notes to Bunny Blanchard? Why this emphasis on the first week of August? That's less than two weeks away.

The senior editor pulled into his driveway at precisely midnight. Margaret was poised behind the front door. She opened it when she heard her husband pull in.

As he walked up the garden path, she knew it was not just another day at the office.

# Chapter 25

I decided to call Marilyn on Sunday.

I thought she'd be home. I let the phone ring a dozen times, and then gave up. I read the Sunday *Herald* and discovered that she was at an undisclosed location receiving treatment for a nervous breakdown. So, the rumor-mill was right. It had been going around all week that she had temper tantrums toward the crew and her fellow actors upon returning to the set of Cukor's ill-fated film.

She needed me. I knew this was an exaggerated sense of importance on my part, but I believed it to be true.

*An undisclosed location.*

I pumped up the Chevy and headed for the Beverly Glen Hotel. She'd once told me that when things were really going rotten, her bungalow, always on reserve, was her only retreat. It was a long shot but there were no other options. If she were in a clinic in Santa Barbara or Woodland Hills, I'd never be allowed to see her.

I parked in the general lot and walked the stone pathway to bungalow "C". I looked around to make sure nobody was watching. The curtains were drawn on the two windows that faced the walkway. There was no sound within. I was about to give up, when I heard a piano, ever so softly. The music was the same piece that Marilyn had started to play for me weeks ago at her house. The Bach. I listened until the music stopped. I tapped three times on the door. The little brass portal came open, and I could see her widely, spaced eyes.

"Who's there?"

"It's me, Rory. I thought that you…" Marilyn threw the door open, grabbed me by the shirt, and hauled me over the threshold. My God she was strong. She slammed the door shut, latched the deadbolt, and came into my arms.

"Hold me, Rory, hold me close. I need to be held."

I wrapped my arms around her and gently rocked her.

It is so easy to love even if you're not sure you're being loved back. All it takes are moments of tenderness to realize that loving someone is not a contest: there are no winners or losers. Love just comes to you, and, if it feels real, you don't ask questions.

The world disappeared as the fragrance that was her filled my soul, lifting it skyward. I was on the brink of laughing, when I saw the white, grand piano stuffed into a two hundred-square-foot cottage. She felt my happiness and looked up.

"Come, sit with me, Rory, and let me read to you."

I could tell that she was stoned. There was a half-empty bottle of Jameson on top of the piano and two vials of pills on the bedside table with the tops off. She seemed numb. I was glad I found her, but it only took a few minutes for my paranoia to kick in.

"Are you here alone, or is Ms. Welmen with you? Does your doctor know where you are?"

No response. She moved over to the bed, taking me by the hand. She threw herself down on the satin comforter and scooped up one of her journals. She began to read and created a rhythm that was chant-like. She rocked back and forth on the bed. It was like watching a little girl who had just discovered books. A magic spell fell over her, taking away her pain momentarily.

I fought back tears. I sat on a purple velvet chair next to the bed. I could hear her breathing. I knew there was a good chance someone would burst in, but I didn't care. She chose another poem. The last line—

*... To rest my troubled head on your breast.*

When she finished, she looked at me and patted the comforter, smiling that smile. "Would you let me rest my troubled head on your breast, Rory?"

There was no decision to make. Zombie-like, I laid down beside her. She cuddled into my left arm, nuzzling her head deep into my shoulder and breast. In seconds, she was sound asleep.

Again, the dream that was real descended.

I was too stressed to sleep, even with an angel in my arms. I kept expecting the FBI to mow down the front door, weapons drawn, ready to handcuff me and haul me away. The longer she remained peacefully asleep, the better I felt about trying to find her. If this was any indication, I was right to seek her out.

She was calm. Her face had a glow that couldn't be described. Words could not capture her expression, sculpted from marble, painted on canvas—a melody ringing forever in the ear. It would take all of these forms to recreate her image.

My confidence was running full steam. However, the hero inside me had run off to a safer place.

While Marilyn lay in my arms, my heart pounded so strongly I thought it was going to explode. There was no chance to ask her about the Dahlia. It didn't matter anymore.

Thirty minutes with my arms wrapped around her passed by like five. I didn't want to move out from under her, but I could feel that I'd already been granted a gift by spending the last forty-five minutes uninterrupted.

Marilyn didn't tell me who was with her. My guess was that Evelyn Welmen and Marilyn's doctor were nearby. I may have passed them as I made my way here.

I carefully unwrapped myself and slid off the bed onto the velvet chair. I put on my shoes. I'd forgotten that I had taken them off. My gut feeling was that I should get back to Silver Lake as fast as possible.

My mind was jammed with thoughts and counter thoughts when I noticed her journal on the floor. It had slid off the bed when we settled into our embrace. I picked it up, and four typed pages folded in half fell out. They were copies of an original letter to Lee Strasberg—the one person in the world she trusted completely.

## December 19, 1961
Dear Lee, This letter concerns my future plans… and yours as well since my future as an artist is based on our working together.

In the detailed communication, Marilyn lays out a plan she has been working on for months in her mind about forming an independent production company with Marlon Brando and having Strasberg oversee the creative portion.

She wrote to Lee that she understood the importance of an actor or actress to perform live on a stage in a theater, that actors needed to experience the discipline of the theater and to become aware of the need to constantly hone their craft: to become a better vessel. Performing on a stage in front of an audience is real acting. Films require a different technique. Theater is live: there are no second takes. It is this challenge alone that builds a mature artist.

Further thoughts on the importance of discipline and follow-through end the letter.

On a separate page, she lays out a financial budget analysis and lists potential locations for the site in the greater Los Angeles area.

Marilyn—the business tycoon.

It was time to go. I'll be damn lucky if I'm not caught trying to escape. I didn't want to leave but had to.

I placed the copy of the letter back in her journal and left it on the chair. As much as I wanted to, it wouldn't be a good idea to leave her a note. Someone might intercept it. I stood behind the bungalow door fearing to open it. I glanced back at Marilyn, and then walked out, closing the door softly.

As I headed out, I spotted Welmen and Donahue. I guessed right. Her entourage would not leave her unattended for very long. They had only seen me once, and that was weeks ago. I didn't take any chances. There was a labyrinth of pathways on the hotel grounds. They were talking while walking. I veered off to the right, out of their line of vision, and circled back to my car.

Sunset Boulevard is one of the longest streets of any city in the United States. I drove back to my apartment all the way on Sunset wondering if she was okay. It took one hour. I was on autopilot. I arrived without any recollection of the drive.

After locking my garage, I had the strangest feeling that I would never see her again: the time allotted to me was at an end. She would become a precious series of memories that I would carry to the grave.

I tried to shake this feeling as I stood on the porch searching for my key. I heard the phone ringing. I threw the door open and dove for it.

It was Weisman. He said. "Are you sitting down?"

The conversation with my boss was one-sided. He spoke, I listened.

He had been trying to find the source of the photos and the possible mole in our office. He was convinced that Hoover and his crew stole the Dahlia papers and then returned them. Weisman was putting two and two together and coming up with more than four. He believed Hoover applied pressure in the beginning because I was Huey Long's grandson. The head of the FBI had a vast memory for people, places, and events. But even the habit of Hoover to hold a grudge did not explain why he wanted him to shut down my Dahlia assignment. Hoover claimed the Bureau was doing their own investigation and that independent research might jeopardize their efforts.

That didn't make much sense.

What if there was a much larger picture? Is it possible that Hoover was trying to protect someone close to home base who could be implicated in the brutal murder fifteen years ago? Is it conceivable that throughout the subsequent years, the killer has been protected for fear that, if he were known, the secretive, undercover agencies sponsored by our government would come tumbling down like the proverbial house of cards?

I was all ears.

"Listen, Rory, when you first went through the files, do you remember the name of the Hollywood Detective whose father was a doctor?"

"Yeah, it was Detective Malcolm Stoddard from the Hollywood precinct, who was transferred to another case the following day."

Weisman was silent for a few moments. I could hear the sound of papers being shuffled.

"Well, well, well, what do we have here? You are definitely on the right trail, my friend. Stoddard's father was a prominent plastic surgeon who remodeled the faces of the Hollywood elite, nip and tuck."

I got excited. "You don't suppose that this doctor is the one who did the deed? Could I have been right on this one, chief?"

Weisman let out a long breath. "Well, my junior news hound, it's beginning to look a lot like Christmas in July. Gifts are being thrown from Santa's sleigh right into our laps. But don't forget granddad on the other end of the line. When you first brought in your article to me, I told you that my inclination was leaning toward the medical community when the murder first hit the news."

I gulped. "Jesus Christ, boss, if we're both right…"

Weisman cut me off. "We both may be dead in a few hours. Listen up, son, if you and I could figure this out now, then the big chiefs knew about this at the time it happened, and they shut the case down, throwing the scent in another direction. The hounds went one way while the doctor vanished."

Weisman paused. "I pulled a file on all of the articles the *Herald* had printed that focused on local physicians with Hollywood social connections. Good ole' doc Stoddard was mentioned quite regularly. He retired and moved to Europe shortly after Liz Short's mutilated body was discovered. He hasn't been heard from since."

I could hear Weisman striking a match. "I'm thinking that the good doctor had heavy pull beyond local politics."

My throat was dry. I squeaked out my next words. "Do you really think someone is out to get us? To make us disappear?

Weisman chuckled. "Well, my young friend, there are certainly a lot of Houdini's out there with plenty of tricks up their sleeves."

He became silent. "Allan, you still there?"

"Yeah, kid, I was just thinking that we should continue this conversation in person and not on the phone. Meet me at the paper in one hour. My office."

He hung up without saying goodbye.

My afternoon with Marilyn left me exhausted. It was eight o'clock and I hadn't had anything to eat since breakfast. I rode the squeaky elevator to the sixth floor. I could see a light on in his office. A few of the night team journalists were at their desks.

I knocked.

"Entre, mon ami." Weisman had a plate of sandwiches, a bowl of potato salad, and six beers on top of his desk. "I thought you might be a little hungry after your afternoon nap with Monroe." He smiled ear to ear. "Not to panic. Donahue saw you scurrying away. He called to tell me you made it out safely. It's just between the three of us."

I grabbed a sandwich, opened a beer, and downed most of the bottle in seconds. "Jesus, can't a guy do anything in this town without the world knowing about it?"

Weisman took a bite of potato salad and washed it down with a half-bottle. "Sure, damn near anyone can get away with anything unless they happen to be hanging around with the most popular figure in the world. Then, chances are they're going to be spotted."

He shoved two hand-written notes over to my side of the desk. As I read them, still munching full speed ahead, he filled me in. "It seems as though your favorite Columnist, the creator of *Woman's Day*, has been smooching in dark places with Monroe's watchdog, Evelyn Welmen."

He paused to let out a belch, "Actually, it's a little bit more serious than a lesbian relationship right on our doorstep. They both appear to be aware of, and possibly working for, that secretive faction I referred to, which means there may be a plan in the works to harm someone we're both very fond of."

I gasped. "You mean, Marilyn?"

"Bingo, you win the sweepstakes." He popped open another beer and lit a cigarette. I held up my hand. He lit another one and handed it to me. "I'm only guessing, but I think this ties into the Dahlia case, and that 'mistake' mentioned in the notes, I believe, refers to the photos."

"It's a long shot, but it seems feasible to me, with the facts gathered up so far, that one of the members of this group or faction or secret society…or whatever, went out of their way to impress the others by arranging for the photos. But the stunt backfired.

"That's why only the *Herald* was given the gift of your intimate moments in living, extra grainy, black-and-white photos." Weisman stared at the ceiling.

"The plan was probably some kind of a leverage play to keep the paper in line with God knows what. The world gets more ridiculous every day."

My appetite was gone. "But, who are these people?"

"Who the hell knows? But I'll bet you dollars to donuts that this organization is buried deeper into our government than the FBI and the CIA put together.

Weisman rubbed his eyes and looked at his watch. "It's after nine o'clock on a Sunday night and I should be home, with my slippers on, getting soused with my wife and watching Jackie Gleason and Ed Sullivan."

We sat in silence, having a tough time wrapping our thoughts around these latest developments.

Weisman stood to put on his hat and coat. "If you noticed, Evelyn refers to 'the group' on both of the notes to Blanchard. One thing was for sure: this *group* might outrank Hoover and his playmates. That is definitely something to think about."

He opened the door for us both. "Starting tomorrow, I'm doing some serious research." He grinned.

"That is, if I haven't forgotten how."

# Chapter 26

**Driving home, I realized how stupid and naïve I'd been.** I took so much for granted, thinking anything was possible. Has that been my downfall?

The walk from my garage to the front door gave me a chill. I was beyond exhaustion and my imagination was running wild. I thought I could see shadowy figures lurking in the Hydrangeas. I was sure the avocado tree was full of assassins dressed in black ready to swoop down on me. I ran to my apartment and entered, out of breath.

I needed to cool down, put the past few weeks into prospective. The problem was that living in the vacillating reality of Hollywood, I didn't stand a chance of making sense out of any of this mess.

For the first time since meeting Marilyn, I wished I never had. I scolded myself the minute that thought crossed my mind.

What if I hadn't written the review of Sandburg's poetry? She never would have called and thus we would have never met. Then, I asked myself, would I trade my time spent with her for anything else?

Okay, so, line me up and shoot me. I've lived the part of life that counts.

And besides, none of this was our fault. We're two people who found a connection and plugged into it for whatever it was worth. That concept looks good on paper, but will it hold up in tinsel town?

I wasn't sure.

The fact was that I got carried away. It's that simple.

An unbelievable event that no one could have predicted occurred in my life, and I wasn't sure I handled it well. I discovered an intellect buried deeply into a woman whose fame was based on her sex appeal and not her thoughts.

I believe the problem lies with man's inability to look beyond the borders of a persona. How could a sexy movie star also have knowledge of Bartók's music and Marcello Ficino's translations of Plato for Lorenzo de' Medici? When someone has the capacity to do several diverse things, the result on the observer is confusion: a movie star is a movie star, that's all there is to it.

It was two a.m. I hauled my raggedy ass to the bedroom but didn't get undressed. I was so worn out I didn't have the strength to brush my teeth. I stood by the bed and fell into it.

The call woke me at seven thirty on Monday morning. Weisman reminded me that we needed to be at Max Gingold's office this afternoon to sign papers.

I arrived at the newsroom just before nine o'clock. Weisman was not in his office. I sat at my desk feeling like the living dead when Carol passed by, bubbly as she sorted the mail.

"You two just blow in from an all-night poker game?" She paused. "You look worse than the chief. What gives?"

I pushed my chair back feeling dizzy. "That's right: a poker game, and the stakes, as you've guessed, were high."

Carol twisted her body in a funny way as she turned to leave. "Well, I hope you didn't lose your shirt?"

I checked to see if I had mine on. I did, and luckily, there wasn't any blood on it. I needed caffeine desperately.

In a few hours, I would be in the same room with Marilyn, assuring those gathered there, that all we did was tell the truth. Somehow, I had the feeling that truth didn't matter. That after all the parties involved signed off on whatever legal documents her team had dreamed up, then everything and everyone would evaporate right there in the middle of Century City.

I arrived at Gingold, Snell and Walters, and was buzzed through. The appointments secretary, seated stiffly in her chair, looked askance at me, as if I should be accompanied by a parent. I told her my name, and she perked up.

"Why, yes, Mr. Long, you are expected. I'm afraid there is a small delay, but we hope you'll be comfortable." With a forced smile, she extended her left arm, slowly sweeping it through the air, indicating the couches and chairs available in the circular lobby. She reminded me of an airline hostess. There were several doors with brass-embossed nameplates along the paneled walls. Gingold's was the largest.

"Would you like a coffee while you're waiting?"

She asked in a way that begged me to decline her insincere offer.

"No, thank you, not for now. May I smoke? The relieved secretary pointed to several glass ashtrays, again, in the same manner that an airline hostess points out emergency exits.

I was afraid I might run into Marilyn while waiting. If I did, surely my nervous-ninny personality would stumble over a simple hello. Yesterday I held her in my arms, yet I felt that if she saw me before the meeting, she would pretend she didn't know me.

Minutes went by like hours. Finally, a buzzer sounded. The Secretary picked up a receiver, nodding as she listened, and then hung up. I never could understand why people did that; the person they're talking to can't see them.

"You may go in now." She headed for the door with the biggest brass nameplate, knocked twice, and opened it, repeating that airline-hostess sweeping gesture.

Attorney Gingold's office was huge and cluttered. Three of the four walls were floor to ceiling books. The room was dimly lit, offering a soothing atmosphere. I imagined that many on Gingold, Snell and Walter's client list needed the calm environment.

Gingold was seated at a massive, modern, tubular-steel-and-smoked-glass desk, smiling that corporate smile with his hands folded in front of him. It took a few seconds for my eyes to adjust to the dim light. Weisman was sprawled upon a brown leather sofa to the left of Gingold, smoking and smiling. Seated next to him was whom I assumed to be one of the paper's corporate attorneys. I didn't know him. We nodded.

Marilyn, wearing huge, dark sun glasses, a mauve-colored, man's dress shirt and a pair of jeans, was seated in a Moroccan-red leather wingback chair to the right of the ever-smiling attorney. A white sweater was draped over her shoulders. She seemed frozen in place, staring off, unaware of the others.

I could tell this was going to be a fun way to end the day.

Weisman addressed me. "How's it going, kid? You find this place easy enough?"

I knew he was kibitzing in an attempt to lighten the moment. "Just fine, boss, thanks for asking, and no problem finding the front door."

Gingold jumped right in. Time was money. "Alright, let's see if we can complete the signing and filing of documents concerning the articles encompassing interviews sanctioned by Ms. Monroe and conducted by Rory Daniel Long, an employee of the Los Angeles *Herald Examiner*."

Gingold acknowledged the attorney from our team. "As we all have busy schedules, I propose that we move along with the official explanations, agreements, and signatures required."

Our attorney gave a quick nod to Gingold. I had to assume this guy wasn't much of a talker.

Marilyn's personal representation in all matters legal pushed a button, and two women entered within seconds carrying file folders. They spread them out in some pre-arranged order on his desk. While doing this, both women glanced over toward the star, hoping for a greeting. They exited disappointed.

After the door shut, Marilyn shocked everyone by requesting a few minutes alone with me. Weisman, Gingold, and the quiet man left the office.

Marilyn removed her sunglasses. Her eyes were red and her face looked swollen, carved with wrinkles I'd never noticed. She said nothing. She held out her hand. I took it. She led me over to her chair. I sat on the matching ottoman. She kept my hand in hers. She wouldn't look me in the eyes.

"Rory, I'm so sorry for the way I've treated you. It's just that my life has been…"

I broke in. "You have nothing to apologize to me for. As a matter of fact, it's I who owe you an apology."

She looked up with a startled expression.

I continued. "You have been nothing short of wonderful to me. I'm sorry that I'm not old enough or powerful enough to take away your pain. I feel helpless toward you, the person I would most like to help."

She smiled and brushed a tear away from her right eye. "My, my, you are forever the gallant knight." She started to breathe again, letting her body sink into the chair. "Can you give me a cigarette?"

I lit two and grabbed an ashtray. I knew she had something to tell me that wasn't going to be easy to say. Of course, my mind traveled the distance taking in anything and everything that could possibly involve me in her life. Then I gave up and waited for her to speak.

She smoked languidly; as if this was her first cigarette and she wanted to know how she looked holding it—like a teenager. Halfway down, she snubbed it out. She spoke the minute it was dead.

"They aren't going to publish our interviews." She stared at the floor, hunched over and resting her arms on her legs. "They feel that if the world discovers that I have a brain in my head, my career will be finished." She looked up and smiled. "Funny, I thought that was an already established fact." She started to laugh and broke out crying.

I went into action. I moved closer to her and wrapped my arms around her. She began to cry heavily. It was loud enough for the others to come through the door. My family gene kicked in. "We'll call you when we need you, now go away!"

The three men looked at each other in astonishment and retreated. I took charge.

"What do you mean, *they* will not allow the articles to be printed? What do *they* have to do with it? Is Weisman in on this?"

My anger and frustration was building. Who in the hell do these people think they were?

Marilyn had let it all out. She calmed down. "The heads at Twentieth became aware of our interviews two weeks ago. I'm not sure how. I was hoping we could just do this and no one would say anything." She looked up at me like a helpless orphan.

I sat there wondering what this was all about. Of course, I knew the answer before the question. If you are a person of principles and foolish enough to plant yourself in this evil garden passing under the name of Hollywood, you'll spend most of your time tangled in weeds that grow faster than you can pull them. It is the sad comedy of our existence.

The room took on an eerie silence. We sat close to one another, staring into each other's eyes searching for an answer.

The door opened abruptly and the three men reentered, accompanied by Donahue and Welmen. Weisman waggled his hand near his leg to get my attention. He knew what I was thinking. He shook his head rapidly with a dour expression: the *not now* signal.

I took his cue and joined him and the quiet man on the couch. Evelyn was fussing over Marilyn. Donahue was preparing to speak.

"Rory, everyone in this room is aware of your recently formed friendship with Marilyn and her equally matched return."

Donahue looked at Weisman. "I've known your boss for a number of years and have always admired his ethics in what is one of the toughest games in town: telling the public what goes on in their world."

His attention shifted back to me. "Allan showed me your articles, and they are first rate. You can imagine that I have proofed hundreds of interviews and articles for fan magazines over the years I've been in Ms. Monroe's employ."

He sat on the edge of Gingold's desk beaming down at me.

"You have the makings of a damn fine writer, kid, and if you decide to stay the course, I think, at least in my humble opinion, that you'll have one hell of a future ahead of you." His expression became taut. "Unfortunately, for several reasons and decisions handed down from various powerful persons with a vested interest in the star's future, it is not feasible to print the results of your joint efforts at this time."

Marilyn had put her sunglasses back on and stared into space. Donahue moved off the desk and knelt in front of her. He grasped her hands and said softly. "The time will come when the world will have the chance to discover your other life. I know you, and deep within, you know that this is how it must be for the foreseeable future."

She removed her sunglasses and looked around Jim, at me. "And what about Rory? What about all of his time and effort?"

Gingold stepped up to the plate. "We here at the firm, along with the powers that be, have taken that into consideration and have decided on what we feel to be a fair amount to compensate for the..." The old man coughed. "...The subsequent delay in publishing."

Weisman did what he does best. "Well, folks, it's going on five thirty, and me, I'm for signing whatever papers need to be signed and heading for the Brown Derby to have a bucket of martinis." Weisman gave me a fatherly look. "Shit happens, kid."

I knew Weisman had a lot more to say on the subject, especially the fact that the *Examiner* would not be able to publish the interviews. He was counting on this series, but he knew better than to make a bigger mess now than we already had on our hands.

The quiet man and Gingold had ballpoint pens at the ready near the papers for all parties to sign. It seemed anticlimactic after what it had just occurred. Marilyn signed first and was hustled out of the room by Evelyn. She didn't look at me when she left.

I was numb as I signed a dozen papers without reading them. What did it matter? The world as I had known for the past two months had just exploded.

# Chapter 27

The house she had loved from the moment the real estate agent showed it to her seemed cold and uninviting.

After a few days in the Beverly Glen bungalow, her return to the cozy hacienda didn't offer any joy. Donahue and Evelyn had done their best to keep her spirits up, but she had avoided all of their efforts. Right now, nothing seemed to matter.

She was lonely and feeling beyond her years. She was tired; her mind was weak and unfocused. She needed some time to herself. To get the space she needed, she would have to call upon the actress within.

Even though the house was cold, she opened the French windows and sprawled out on the brown leather couch near the piano.

Evelyn finished unpacking and approached her. "Is there anything I can do for you, dear?"

The director within yelled *take one*.

Marilyn turned to Evelyn with a big smile. "That's very sweet, Eve, but right now I'm just tired and need to take a bath and have a bite to eat. I'm starving!"

This was music to Evelyn's ears. Monroe had hardly touched any food the three days she was recuperating in the bungalow. "Great, I'll draw you a bath. Is there anything in particular you'd like to have?"

The film was still rolling.

"Oh, Eve, would you be sweet enough to go to the deli in Brentwood and bring back two pastramis on rye, a bucket of coleslaw, and two crème sodas?" Marilyn stood and gave her a hug. Her smile worked its charm. Evelyn ran into the bathroom to run a bath.

Jim Donahue was on the phone the minute they arrived. He had a good relationship with his boss; she always listened to his advice and sometimes even followed it. The living room was cold. Jim shut the French doors and sat down beside Marilyn, on the couch.

"Tell me, honey, what's that Rory Long guy to you? He seems like a nice kid, and he can definitely write, but what gives between you two? I'm just curious."

"He represents the beginning of history."

Donahue looked puzzled.

She cast her eyes down and smiled. "I know it's hard for you to understand a statement like that, but it's true. He marks the beginning of a new cycle. He enjoys giving more than taking. This is new to me."

Marilyn stood gazing around the room as if she were visiting it for the first time. "He is a born writer who utilizes heart, mind, and soul." She giggled. "Although he's really skinny."

Donahue smiled, but he wasn't finished with his fact gathering. "Look, hon, I know you've spent some intimate time together, but you haven't….you know…"

Marilyn gave her press agent a sultry look. 'Well, as a matter of fact, we've slept together twice."

Jim was about to respond.

"And what I mean is we've gone to sleep in each other's arms. No sex! That's why he represents a new history for men in my life. He is thoughtful and respectful of women.

She gave a little smirk. "Don't get me wrong. I know all of the signs and I'm sure he'd love to bed me down, but he hasn't pushed for that to happen. Do you get it? He's a man I can trust in the same way that I trust you and Lee."

Donahue slapped his knees and stood up. 'Well, that's certainly a twist." He looked at his watch and then back to Marilyn. "How are you today? I know this has been a rough period. Do you fully understand the reason for pulling the interviews for now?"

The actress surfaced another smile. "Yes, I get it. The timing isn't right with my career in the mess I've made of it. Call Cukor for me and tell him I'll be a good girl from now own."

Marilyn stood and shoved her hands deep into her jeans pockets, turning on that tomboy charm that made men feel at ease around her.

Donahue gathered up his things. "I've got to be running. I have a deadline to make on that *Hollywood Reporter* article about your being hard at it on Cukor's set." He turned around abruptly at the front door. "Are you really as miserable as I think you are?"

The star quit acting.

"Yes. I never could fool you, but I'm going to be okay. I promise." She crossed her heart and smiled fondly at Jim.

Donahue grabbed his hat and coat and sped out of the house. "Tell Eve goodbye for me and that I'll be in touch in the morning. Don't forget you need to be at Paramount by nine o'clock sharp!" He paused keeping his eyes locked on hers and gave her a big smile. "On second thought, I'll have a limo here to pick you up at eight fifteen!'"

Marilyn leaned on the front door and stuck out her tongue. Jim laughed as he got jogged to his car.

Evelyn was putting on her gloves and gathering up her purse and coat. "Your bath is ready. I'm heading out to the deli. Is there anything else you need while I'm there?"

"No, I think the deli will do it. Thanks, Eve, thanks a lot."

Marilyn watched both cars disappear. When the noise stopped, she closed the door. An eerie silence took over. She could not recall being alone in the house before. Everything was still, calm.

She retrieved a shoebox hidden away in her bedroom closet and carried it into the front room as if it contained precious treasure. It did. All nine of her journals, kept over a ten-year period. She opened one at random, reading from it as if a stranger had written down the thoughts on it. Until Rory came into her life, there was no need to travel over past emotional paths, both smooth and rough. Disappointed that the interviews were not going to be published soon, she wanted to catch up with herself by searching for the answer to the most pressing question on her mind: how do I get past the pain?

A bottle of Whisky was nearby. It was time for a tumbler. The warm liquid created a smooth connection between her mind and heart. She was on a cloud trying to find herself—her true self.

So much of what she longed for was centered on self-discipline. Her analysts had attempted to help her with this, but she always felt like she was being scolded as if she were a child.

A line from one of her poems stuck out.

*Loneliness, be still.*

Yes, that is a good thing to remember—to be calm in your separation from the world around you. That's what you get for not liking people in the first place.

That thought brought out a smile. It was true. She couldn't stand to be in a packed room; press conferences were the worst. She felt claustrophobic during the questioning and longed to escape to her hotel room, where she would turn out all the lights and sit in the quiet darkness. That was how she recharged her batteries.

After shooting all day with dozens of people around her, from the technicians to the actors to the executives on the set, she would run to her trailer, lock the door, and put a lamp on the table to read. Then, her breathing would return to normal and even slow down. Yes, she thought she was happiest with a pile of books nearby and some good music playing softly. This was her personal heaven: a place she never dreamed she could share with anyone, until Rory came along.

# Chapter 28

The last time I had seen Marilyn was in Gingold's office.

That was over a week ago. Since then, I'd thrown myself into the Black Dahlia. The stark reality that the interviews would not be in print soon, and perhaps never, had stifled my energy.

She cried her eyes out that day, but how did she really feel? Was she disappointed? Did she even care any more about revealing her other life, the one that she said meant the most to her?

Sometimes, a lost cause is not worth wasting time on. Marilyn had called upon me to write her story, and that was enough to continue my life as a journalist.

The problem was that I needed to talk to Marilyn. I knew by the way she reacted when I first told her about the Dahlia assignment that she was hiding something. She'd told me they'd met one another at the Hollygrove orphanage when Marilyn was doing one of her visits.

Part of me wanted the confirmation for my research. The other part just wanted to be with her one more time.

I had to take the chance. I sat at my desk in the newsroom staring at the phone for twenty minutes, and then I dialed.

Marilyn answered with a groggy voice, barely audible. "Yes…hello?"

I was afraid to speak. "Marilyn, it's me, Rory."

"Hello…Rory, is that you?" She tried to find more energy but seemed detached from it all, as if she wasn't sure of whom she was talking to.

"Marilyn, its Rory. I had to call to see how you were." That was, of course, a lie. I was concerned about her condition, but I really wanted information. I realized at this moment how deceitful I could be. A shiver filled my body. I was becoming a journalist.

She whispered a reply. "Can you come over? I'm all alone. Everyone has abandoned me. It's so cold in the house. Could you come and build a fire?"

It was a late July heat wave. A Santa Ana filled the air with dry desert breeze. It must have been over ninety. She was definitely stoned. I knew that it would be impossible to trust her claim of being alone. I tried to skirt around the issue.

"Well, it's really hot downtown. Where are you in the house—are you in bed?"

Silence. The phone went dead. When the dial tone came on, I began to hyperventilate. Without thinking, I grabbed my jacket and ran to the parking lot.

I pulled onto the gravel driveway. Small, white stones spewed off the tires in all directions as my Chevy squealed to a stop. She may have been telling the truth; there were no other cars around. I had a foreboding feeling.

Everything was too still, too quiet. I knocked on the front door, barely contacting it with my knuckles. My slight rap, aided by the desert winds, opened it. It had been ajar. I stepped in and called out. "Marilyn, I'm here—are you here?"

Nothing.

I moved to the center of the living room, standing like a statue for a few seconds. Suddenly, her figure oozed around the corner of the hallway wrapped in a bed sheet. She drifted over in a somnambulistic fog, throwing her arms around me, the sheet falling to the floor.

To say that I was now in a situation that I had no idea how to handle would be more than accurate. There was definitely only the two of us here. I supported her nude body so she wouldn't collapse. Her hard nipples dug into my breast. I couldn't let myself go, couldn't fondle her to feel her shape, trace my hands along the curves of her body. I was too nervous. My car was out front. I knew that someone would be showing up soon.

I closed my eyes, bent down to the floor and picked up the sheet. She was very stoned. There were several prescription drug vials perched on top of the piano with the lids off.

A spellbinding look came over her. She stood not more than a foot away from me, stark naked, and watched my reaction. I was mesmerized.

"Don't feel embarrassed, Rory, I want you to see me as I am: a woman, not a goddess, nothing special."

I was sweating. My dick had a mind of its own. It grew so hard it was ready to burst through my pants, and there was no way to hide it. She looked down at my crotch, taking my right hand and placing it on her left breast.

She kept her eyes glued to mine, and then she did the unbelievable: her right hand gently unzipped my pants. She reached in and began to massage my cock while smiling in an angelic fashion. She pulled it out and looked down at it while continuing the up and down motion, barely applying any pressure with her fingers.

She massaged the head of my dick with her thumb.

It was the most bizarre sexual encounter imaginable.

As her right hand gently floated along the length of my member in a smooth, up-and-down motion, her body danced in rhythm.

I was in another world.

The room grew dark, and, within seconds, I exploded. She grabbed the back of my neck with her free hand and pulled me into a kiss, exploring my mouth with her tongue while continuing the message until I was completely spent.

When she finished, she fell onto the couch.

I grabbed the sheet off the floor and covered her quickly. I was so embarrassed and afraid at the same time that I panicked. She began to sing a song that made no sense. I zipped up and raced for the front door to get the hell out of there.

I was worried about her but too scared to hang around.

My heart was beating so fast I thought I was going to die. The top was down. I dove into the driver's seat from the passenger side, cranked up the Chevy, and tore out of the driveway.

Two blocks away, I spotted Evelyn's car racing toward the house. I stopped and watched through my rearview mirror.

Who was I kidding?

I made a U turn. Some switch inside me was thrown. I was no longer weak and afraid. I cleaned myself up with a towel I kept in the Chevy for the windows, and raced back.

I bolted through the front door, expecting to be yelled at, but, to the contrary, Evelyn looked at me sympathetically, holding Marilyn's hands. "She's been crying out for you." She told Marilyn I was here. "What is going on between you two? Why are you so important to her?"

I couldn't answer that question with any authority.

During the past few weeks of knowing her, I was never sure where I stood. Sometimes my confidence told me that she truly cared for me. Most of the time, I felt on the outside, looking in.

What transpired between us a few minutes ago had me in a daze, like a waking dream. My guilt was sidelined even though I thought I might have taken advantage of the situation. She made the moves, and I was too weak to resist.

Evelyn motioned me over to the couch. I crouched down and took Marilyn's hands. "I'm here… are you okay now?"

She opened her eyes, swollen from crying. She looked ghastly—no, ghostly. She seemed to be drained of any life force, like a vampire in the making. "Rory, stay with me, okay?"

I wasn't sure if she remembered what had happened or if it would suddenly strike her, causing her to panic. I looked over at Evelyn, who was now joined by the stars personal physician, a doctor Greenstreet.

The doctor, who was at least fifty pounds overweight, bent down to whisper something in Marilyn's ear. She let go of my hands, and he motioned for me to join him on the other side of the room. I followed him out into the garden. He lit a cigarette. "Young man, I understand that you're the journalist who was sanctioned by Ms. Monroe to do a series of articles for the *Examiner* based on interviews. Is that correct?"

I nodded in the affirmative, unable to focus on anything but the sex that had taken place a few minutes ago.

The doctor tossed his half-smoked cigarette into the bushes. "Well, young man, I ask you to stay in touch with her staff, particularly Donahue, and to be available at a moment's notice. Is that possible? Do you have any problem with this request?"

There must be anxiety in the Monroe camp. Were they concerned about her mental stability, to the point that she may attempt suicide? I assured the doctor that I would be on call and gave him my phone number.

When we went back into the house, Donahue arrived. He took me aside and basically gave me the same talk. I gave him my home phone and told each of them that they could reach me at the paper during business hours.

Evelyn brought Marilyn a robe. She was sitting up on her own and sipping a cup of coffee when I left Donahue. She patted the space next to her on the couch. I sat down, not knowing what to say or how to act. This whole scenario was mind-boggling.

What in the hell had just happened? I could only surmise that, after her crew witnessed her demand to be alone with me at Gingold's office, they had reached the conclusion that I meant something to the film star. At least for now.

Marilyn was coming back to herself. I waited in nervous anticipation. Was she going to recall our sexual moment, less than an hour ago, and announce it to the world?

Evelyn arrived with scrambled eggs, toast, and fresh coffee for both of us.

Marilyn spoke to the others in a calm voice. "I would like a few moments with Rory.

Would you mind?"

Without hesitation, they went into the kitchen. Marilyn took a bite of eggs and a sip of coffee before she spoke. "Well, my Arthurian knight returns for another rescue."

She giggled in a way that melted my heart. I smiled at her, unable to come up with any response.

She sensed this and began to laugh. "Tongue-tied, Mr. Journalist?"

My insides were heaving like a volcano. "Beyond that. Look, I don't know what came over me when you…we…"

She held her index finger vertically in front of her lips to indicate silence. "I wanted to do that, Rory. You have nothing to feel guilty about." She smiled a sad smile. "I won't tell you to forget it. That wouldn't be nice."

A shadow fell across her face. She looked confused. She swiveled slightly on the couch to face me. "You know, I always feel good when you're around, even when I'm at my lowest. I need to tell you something."

I had no idea where this was going. I assumed my Alfred E. Newman, *what, me worry* smile, and waited for the punch line.

She caught on, knowing me as she did, but didn't react. She went straight to it. "I hadn't planned on what happened earlier. I just wanted you to see me as a human being. It is so hard to be idolized by millions of strangers who don't have any idea who you are."

She set down her coffee cup and bore into my eyes. "In some strange and funny way, I think I'm in love with you."

I froze.

"Not in the way that I've thought of love in the past but in a new way: a way that I've never experienced before." She touched my breast with her hand. "I love the inside of you, that part that makes up the real you, the one who is there for me even when I am a bitch. There has never been a man in my life who could tolerate both sides of me. You've done this, and therefore I have found a new way to love and be loved."

I remained frozen in place.

Were my ears deceiving me? Was the world's most eminent female film star telling me she loved me? Words finally came. "There isn't anything I wouldn't do for you that's within my power."

Marilyn smiled a teenage smile and bent over to kiss my cheek. She squeezed my hand, and then returned to her eggs and toast. "I'm starving, aren't you?"

Donahue stuck his head around the dining room door and asked if it was all clear. Marilyn motioned with her arm for the troops to enter.

Just like that, we were back to square one, business as usual.

The phone rang. It was Cukor's office. Donahue talked fast and loud on the line. Dr. Greenstreet took Marilyn's pulse, and Evelyn brought out some clothes for Marilyn to choose from for the rest of the day.

I said good-bye. Marilyn made the hand signal to call her. She mouthed the word, "Soon."

I drove back to work along Third Street. It took nearly forty-five minutes. I was hoping to come to some kind of conclusion as to what had just happened in the space of three hours on a Tuesday afternoon—the reason and purpose for my life having crossed hers.

Once again, I reached for the moon and missed.

# Chapter 29

*Saturday afternoon*
*August 4th, 1962*

I was hard at it. The Black Dahlia case had come to the forefront of the public eye due to a leak about the FBI's recent reinvestigation. Weisman was jumping for joy. Although we were still licking our wounds over the denial to print my interviews with Marilyn, we could now go full force with my Dahlia research to reveal the possible implication of a popular, Hollywood medical personality in the brutal murder of a young aspiring actress. There was nothing Hoover could do short of making us disappear—so far, so good.

The phone rang. It was Weisman. "Listen up. I want your final drafts of all the Dahlia articles on my desk Monday morning. I want to go through everything personally during the week. I'm thinking of scheduling the first article for the Monday, August sixth morning edition."

I couldn't help but smile as he went on. He sounded fired up, and Allan Weisman hitting on all cylinders was a great thing to behold.

At two o'clock, I was typing my final draft. I was feeling relaxed for the first time in days. I couldn't take my mind off Marilyn, but the concentration required to edit and analyze my efforts for the Dahlia articles allowed some relief.

I'd worked hard today, so I took myself out to dinner and went to see one of Marilyn's movies I hadn't seen: *The River of No Return,* with Robert Mitchum. I was glued to the screen. It was pure magic. She could depict that undertow of innocence coupled to a life ventured off the straight and narrow path so well. I topped off the evening by stopping into the Polo Lounge for a martini. Willy was there; he greeted me with a huge smile. As I sipped my drink, it struck me that, until tonight, I hadn't watched any of her films since we met. I had the real thing in front of me and didn't need to view the larger-than-life image on a screen.

I woke up later than usual on Sunday. Birds were singing in a frenzy. I hadn't noticed how loud they could get until this moment. I wanted to call Marilyn, just to say hello. No, that's a lie. I wanted to tell her that I loved her too and was hoping she would speak those three transforming words again. I stared at the phone for a few minutes and decided to wait until the afternoon. It was already eleven a.m. There were a least two more hours needed to complete the polishing of my Dahlia series. I took a brief hike around the neighborhood and got back just past noon. With a peanut-butter-and-jelly sandwich in one hand, I pecked out the rest of my editing feeling as if the weekend had been perfect. All I needed now was to hear her voice.

Just after two o'clock in the afternoon, my phone rang for the first time. As I got up to answer it, I made a bet with myself that it was either Weisman or Marilyn. I held out a small percentage on the possibility that Rose was calling from Colorado.

It was Weisman. He was frantic. "Rory, I'm sorry to tell you this, but Marilyn was just discovered dead from an overdose in her home. Thirty minutes ago." That's all I remember. The next thing I knew, I was prone on my couch being attended to by paramedics. I had passed out when I heard the news. Weisman had sent an emergency squad to my apartment. The front door was off. I thought I was dreaming. When I came to, Weisman stood over me, smiling.

"You okay, kiddo?

The horror of the phone call came back. I tried to get up but fell back onto the couch. Everything was in slow motion. "Is she…are you sure she's dead?"

Weisman took my right hand, squeezed it between his hands, and confirmed that she had passed on. "I'm so sorry, Rory, but it's true. She's gone."

I began to cry my eyes out. The emergency medical unit was packing up, and my landlord, along with his son, was putting my front door back on the hinges. I sat up, and Weisman sat down beside me.

He ordered me to take a few days off. Weisman advised me to disappear for a while. There was no reason to go to print with the Dahlia report. The next few weeks would be taken up with Marilyn's so-called suicide. Weisman calculated that I would be deluged with journalists and press as soon as they put two and two together and started to investigate the last few weeks of her life: what she did and who she did it with. They were bound to connect the dots and discover our relationship.

I agreed to lay low without knowing why. I put myself into the hands of an experienced person who had dealt with the public his entire life. I was numb. I knew I was hurting, but I wasn't sure how much, until days later. I felt guilty for not calling her that morning; I could have said something that would have prevented this tragedy. Why was I so hesitant and unconfident? For Christ's sake, she told me she loved me! I broke down again, and Weisman patted me on the back. "There's nothing we can do now, sport. Are you going to be okay by yourself tonight?" I stood up and looked around. Everything in my apartment looked foreign to me. Nothing seemed familiar. "Yeah, I'll be fine. Can't thank you enough for all of this."

Weisman stood up and gave me an inquisitive look. "I'm heading to the paper downtown. The news media is in third gear racing for coverage on her death."

I asked him if I could be of any help. He told me to stay put and try to get some sleep. Monday morning will be here before you know it. He scuffed my hair and smiled as he turned to leave. "I'll call you in an hour or so to see how you're doing. Get some rest."

Suddenly, all was still. I was alone, and the apartment was draped in silence.

When a public figure passes away, no matter what the circumstance, the average person is affected to one degree or another. People mourn for a brief period before they find new focus. When a major film star like Marilyn Monroe dies in such a shocking fashion, she takes a piece of her fans with her. An empty space is created which can never be filled.

For me, it was different. I had shared the last two months of her life. We had communicated with each other on various levels, both mental and emotional. I knew her intimately. She told me that she loved me a few days before her death; the term has many definitions, but I knew how she meant it, and it was real.

The next few days were a blur.

An autopsy had been ordered, and sure enough, there were enough drugs in her to kill her. Pundits from every corner were arguing over the cause of the star's demise. Some were calling for a complete investigation, not buying the suicide report. An abundance of conspiracy theories were put forth. The coroner could not be reached, and the funeral was due up in a few days.

Now the question was, did she do it to herself, or was she injected with the overdose of drugs that cost her her life?

Rose called me from Boulder wanting to know if I'd like her to fly out and keep me company or if I'd like to come home for a while. I told her I'd get back to her when I could. At that time, I wasn't sure when that would be.

It was extremely difficult to recount that period of time after her death. I'd tried, over and over, to sit quietly and attempt to remember the events that took place after her death. But my memory had retained very little. My awareness of being alone in the world took precedence over everything else that happened. I felt completely alone without her, and still do to this day.

I was on paid leave from the paper. A few days after her death, I drove to the Beverly Hills Hotel. I wasn't sure why; I just needed to go there.

I strolled into the Polo lounge. The bar was empty at two in the afternoon. Willy stood at the far end, staring off into space. He saw me and quickly came over.

"Monsieur, I am so sorry to welcome you here under these circumstances." He offered a short but sincere smile and a courteous bow.

I thanked him for his kindness. "I had to stop by. I'm not sure how long I can stay…you see, I'm not very well."

Willy grabbed my hands.

"None of us are very well young man. Anyone who had the chance to talk with her, joke with her—in short, be around her feels a loss that shall never be retrieved, and I could feel that she held a very important place in her life for you." While he spoke, he made a pitcher of martinis. "Will you join me in a libation in honor of our friend, who has left us alone together?"

He handed me a glass, we clinked and took a sip. I climbed onto a barstool. Willy went to the entrance, posted the *closed* sign, and locked the front door. He returned to his drink with a mischievous expression. "I think we are exceptionally closed for small repairs."

He poured a second drink for each of us, and we saluted one another. "Young man," he began, "I lived through the Second World War in a country that claims neutrality. Switzerland was my place of birth, but I had to leave. My young soul desired adventure and travel. I ended up in New York after the war, and it was Tyrone Power who brought me to California." He paused for a moment, and then asked, "How old are you?"

I told him.

Willy nodded his head as he thought about what he was going to say. "Marilyn was very special. Not because she was a famous personality but because she cared for others even though most of those around her took advantage of her thoughtfulness."

I finished my second martini and knew that I wouldn't be behind the wheel soon. The room was slowly spinning. He made a stiff batch of the cocktails purposely. "Wow, I'm pretty plastered."

He came around the bar and sat beside me. "Not to worry, everything will be hunky-dunky."

The phrase made me laugh. It was the first time I had since Sunday.

Willy waited for me to settle down. Tears mixed with laughter. He squeezed my arm.

"May I tell you a little story?"

His eyes were full of wisdom. I nodded.

"When I was a young man during the Second World War, I had a dear friend from Amsterdam who shared my dream of going to America after the battles were over. His parents were friends of my father and mother, and they had come to visit us for a few days. While staying with us, the news of Nazi bombing raids all over Holland was announced. He and his family rushed back to their home, and that was the end of our friendship until one night in New York, many years later."

A banging on the door interrupted Willy. He went to inform the clients that small repairs were in progress; the bar would be open within the hour.

He returned with a smile. "I was telling the truth: we *are* undergoing small but important repairs, n'est pas?"

We clinked glasses, and he picked up where he left off. "One evening, I believe it was a Saturday night in nineteen fifty, I was managing the restaurant and bar at the St. Moritz Hotel. There was a big event taking place in the main ballroom. During the day, florists arrived with bouquets and special decorations, and a large orchestra setup in the late afternoon. Around twenty musicians filed past my station as I was tallying up receipts.

"My eyes were fixed on a series of numbers when one of the musicians tapped me on the shoulder. I looked up and, to my surprise, there stood my friend from Amsterdam, lugging a huge bass fiddle with him. We both broke out in joyful laughter and hugged each other until we couldn't breathe. It was a fantastic moment."

I was enjoying Willy's story but wasn't sure where it was going. What the hell, I knew that in my condition I wasn't going anywhere. "So, did you guys get together later that night?"

Willy smiled faintly. "Yes, and of course, we picked up our friendship right where we left off. But that is not the heart of the matter." He stared down into the glass for a moment. "I asked my friend about his family, his parents and sister. A look of great sadness came over his face. He told me that, shortly after they returned to Amsterdam, his mother asked him to go to the market to try and find some butter, and when he returned, their house was gone. The Luftwaffe had bombed the neighborhood. His family was wiped out while he was returning from the market."

I looked at Willy's face. He had tears in his eyes. I put my arm on his shoulder. He sighed heavily, and then started to smile.

"But, there was a positive side to this tragedy." Willy checked my face to make sure my second martini hadn't left me unconscious.

"My friend was sixteen years old and had no place to go. He went to the local nightclub that his parents had often visited to go dancing or listen to music. The owner felt sorry for him, so he let him stay there. He helped out to earn his board and keep.

"One night, an orchestra arrived, but the bass player didn't. In the corner of the bar, there was an old bass with three strings leaning against the wall. The owner ordered my friend to play the bass with the band. My friend, of course, had no idea how to play a bass or any other musical instrument. The owner merely shrugged and said, 'fake it.' That night, my friend fell in love with the bass and thus began a career as a musician, and from that night to this, he is still playing professionally in New York."

Willy stood to straighten his tuxedo and adjust his tie. "We lost our friend, but we have work to do. She gave you the passage to be a writer. She gave me her friendship, spreading her magic around every time I was near her."

I stood, feeling less effect from the martinis. "That's a great story, Willy. We have to move on, right?"

I sat back down. There was one more thing I needed to discuss. Willy walked behind the bar and faced me. I hesitated to say what was on my mind. "Willy, do you believe that Marilyn killed herself, or that maybe she was…"

The concierge looked at me sternly and spoke in a whisper. "This is America, and we are encouraged to think on our own, to speak freely on any and all subjects." A woeful look came over him. "But America is part of a world full of good and bad people. We like to think about the good people whenever we can, but bad people are just as likely to influence our lives." The concierge brushed some lint away from his satin tuxedo collar. He smiled at me. "My dear friend, I find it very hard to believe that madam took her own life, but…she had known many bad people."

That was about as good an answer as I could hope for at this moment. Willy walked me to the door. He took out a business card and scribbled something on the back.

"Take this to the dining room and give it to Serge. He will spread a great meal for you along with as much coffee as you need. It's on the house. Stay there as long as you wish. At least until you feel you can drive safely."

We laughed. I gave the little man a hug. "Thanks, Willy, you've been a great help."

He smiled and pinched my cheek. "Don't be a stranger. Take care of yourself." He opened the door to find clients eager to enter. "And thanks to you for the small repairs."

Her funeral was a dreary event attended by shocked mourners stiff in their movements at the grave site. Lee Strasberg delivered a eulogy fit for the queen. He was visibly shaken. Everyone in attendance was speechless.

I ran out before the burial began. Reporters were after me. There was a buzz going around Hollywood about our relationship. I didn't need this. I had learned quickly the disadvantages of public life, from being the grandson of a controversial politician to nurturing an unexpected relationship with the woman of every man's dreams.

It would take years to quell the pain, and I wasn't sure this had been accomplished. The memories of being close to her in proximity, as well as emotionally, continued to haunt me.

After the funeral, I returned to my Silver Lake apartment. I sifted through my notes on our interviews and the pages I had copied out from the two journals that were briefly in my possession.

It was impossible to get over the fact that she was no longer here.

My afternoon spent with Willy helped—just to hear about his boyhood friend's devastating tragedy and survival, as the one left behind.

I felt like the one left behind. For months, every time the phone rang, I thought it could be her.

I went to see all of her movies, over and over, picking out places in the film that reminded me of a gesture she made in my direction when we were together.

It was all too sudden.

It was impossible for my insides to believe that she was truly no longer with us. That was the part that hurt the most. Her death came about on the heels of her telling me she loved me. I knew what she meant by this statement, but love is still love no matter what degree or level you interpret it to be. Selfishly, I wasn't allowed enough time to bask in this glow that was her.

I was aware of my possessiveness. I needed her, and I now believed that she needed me in her collection of complex emotions. It gave me great joy to know that some aspect of my being provided a sliver of happiness and contentment in her life.

Shortly after Marilyn's funeral, I was contacted by Gingold, who informed me that I was mentioned in Marilyn's will.

It hardly registered.

I agreed to meet him at his Century City office after lunch on Monday. I wasn't eating much, so that translated into one o'clock in the afternoon,

I arrived to be greeted by the airline-hostess secretary. This time I was shown right in.

Gingold was all smiles. The red-leather chair Marilyn sat in weeks ago during the meeting was in front of his desk. I felt uncomfortable but went with it. I had no idea if it was placed there on purpose or if he even remembered who sat where that day.

On his desk was a small, pale-blue box with a Tiffany label. There was an envelope underneath it, which looked to be the size of a greeting card.

"This was deposited in my safe by Ms. Monroe over a month ago. She requested that I witness your taking possession of said article, and that you should open it in my presence." Gingold cleared his throat. "I have absolutely no explanation for her request except that it is written here in a memo in her handwriting, if you'd care to see it."

I wasn't sure what to think. I looked up at the attorney after staring at the box.

He followed up. "I know nothing more than you do. It is a genuine Tiffany jeweler's box, and its contents are unknown to anyone except the shop and Ms. Monroe." He reached over and gently shoved the card and the box toward me. He sat back in his chair and steepled his fingers, smiling.

I opened the card first. "Am I required to read to you the contents of the card?"

He shook his head no.

Dearest Rory,

This gift is my design. I hope that you will enjoy it in many ways even though it is unusual. You can keep it as it is forever or break it down and redeem the parts should you need financial aid in the future. I wish I could be with you just to see the expression on your face when you open the box. Take good care of yourself.

Always, with love, Marilyn

I broke down and cried, unable to stop. I could hear her voice as I read. Gingold sat patiently behind his desk while I pulled myself together.

I undid the ribbon and popped the lid. Inside was a small replica of a typewriter, fashioned out of clear and white diamonds. It was stunning. Even

Gingold whistled when he saw it. I honestly didn't know what to think. The object was approximately three square inches in size and heavily detailed.

I was shocked.

She's been gone less than a week and I still can't really feel myself—can't find my center. Gingold and I stared at the object, which shimmered in the light.

He came out of his trance and handed me a certificate of authenticity signed by Tiffany's appraisers, stating the value of the over thirty select diamonds that made up the piece. Collectively, the current market value of the stones amounted to over one hundred thousand dollars.

I understood the card now. If I needed to, I could go to Tiffany's and have her gift disassembled to sell off the diamonds, one at a time. I was in a state of shock, when Gingold cut through the cloud.

"By the way, Rory, I have a feeling that your life will become extremely complicated quite soon. You may need an attorney to handle your business affairs. I know it is not a pleasant subject to bring up so close to Marilyn..." The powerful attorney paused to weigh his words, "leaving us, but clocks don't stop: the world keeps turning. People will be approaching you making demands and offering to pay you for them in return. If, by chance, you haven't secured legal representation for your business affairs, let me know if I can be of assistance."

As I stood to leave, he handed me another envelope. "I was also to give you this note. It is not personal, but it's a copy for you of instructions Ms. Monroe issued, which allows you to take a book from her library at her home: any book of your choosing. Just call Ms. Welmen to make an appointment."

With that, Max Gingold stood to shake my hand and wished me well, slipping a gold-embossed business card into my shirt pocket.

I waved goodbye to the airline-hostess and ran to my car.

I stopped to fill up the tank and headed for Malibu. I had no plan. I drove along the Pacific Coast Highway all the way to Santa Barbara. Once there, I checked into a hotel on the beach, bought some pajamas and a toothbrush, and sat up all night in my room, staring at the diamond miniature typewriter.

The next morning, I cruised slowly back down to Los Angeles. I felt refreshed.

She had thought of me: what else could I ask?

# Chapter 30

Dreading any more emotional trauma, I kept putting off the call to Evelyn to set a date to go to Marilyn's home and pick out a book from her library.

It was three weeks after her passing, and soon, they would be emptying the contents of her house. There was no chance of the hacienda becoming a historical landmark—she hadn't lived there long enough to warrant that classification.

Those in charge of her estate would put all of her belongings in storage until the right moment in time when her possessions could be auctioned off to the highest bidder.

Local and nation-wide press had hounded me. Journalists of all shapes and sizes were trying their best to pluck some secretive gems out of me about our relationship. I refused to talk with any of them. I had no intention of giving a foot up to any columnist seeking higher ground.

My precious Chevy convertible was up for sale on a used car lot in Van Nuys. I was now the proud owner of a non-descript Volkswagen. My nineteen fifty-seven yellow dream was too recognizable after a KTLA media truck chased me down Ventura Boulevard one night as I was leaving Du-par's parking lot. I felt it had to go. One of the waitresses on roller skates at Bob's Big Boy told the press that Marilyn and I had ordered lunch there one day in July. The girl described my car in detail. Absurd as it may sound, collectors were trying to find out what had happened to it. Undoubtedly, there would be a bidding war to own a vehicle that the film star had spent an afternoon in.

The world was coming apart at the seams.

I set a date to meet Evelyn at the hacienda. I wasn't sure I could do it, but I had no choice. She told me they were going to empty the place in two days; it was now or never.

The sound of crunching gravel under the tires of my car as I pulled in made me nauseous. Evelyn came out the front door, not knowing it was me. She was used to the Chevy. I bounced out of the car and waved to relieve her anxiety.

She stood by the entrance, with her arms folded beneath her breasts. She looked haggard and nervous. She had aged considerably since Marilyn's death.

When I approached the front door, she went back inside without saying hello. When I stepped across the threshold, I found her standing near the bookcase, crying. I didn't know what to say. After all, we hadn't exchanged more than a few words in the time I'd known her. "Evelyn, I'm so sorry. Is there anything I can do?"

She grabbed a box of Kleenex that was sitting on the piano, blew her nose, daubed her eyes, and straightened back up. "No, I'm fine, thank you." She turned and gazed at the bookcase. "You are to take any one book you'd like."

Silence. I had a feeling there was something she wanted to tell me but wasn't sure if she should. I waited for a few moments. I could tell she was holding something back, but it never surfaced.

"Evelyn, would it be okay with you if I could be alone while choosing a book. It would mean a lot to me."

She gave me a wistful smile and, without saying anything, went down the hallway.

I was barely holding myself together. The fragrance of Marilyn's Chanel lingered. I half-expected her to walk out from the hall and tell me that her death was just a joke.

Then I recalled what she said when we first started the project: *I don't want to be remembered as a joke.*

I scanned the titles, slowly remembering the interview at the Polo Lounge and the excitement in her voice as she talked about her collections of books.

My legs were getting weak. I hadn't counted on these circumstances to be standing there without her. She should be there. We should be going through the bookcase together. This is not fair. God is not just.

I realized at this moment that the reason I wanted to be alone was to see if I could conjure up her ghost by the magic of imagination. If I could just concentrate hard enough, maybe she would reappear.

I removed Lee Strasberg's book on becoming the total actor, offered to Marilyn soon after they met. His dedication to her was brief. He just wrote, "You've got what it takes—Lee." A surge of emotion shot through me like an injection of adrenaline. I felt dizzy. She certainly had what it takes, and all of it was taken from her—taken from us.

I needed to sit down. The piano bench was nearby.

I stared along the length of the instrument. The thought crossed my mind that a grand piano with the lid closed resembled a coffin. They were probably getting ready to move it into storage. I wished I could own it. I would haul it around with me forever.

The natural temptation to run my fingers along the keys was too strong to resist. I turned over my right hand and placed my index fingernail on the lowest note and swept along the white keys in a slow glissando.

When I reached the notes at the top, there was a thud. It jarred me. I replayed a half-dozen keys near the end of the register, and again, *thud-thud-thud*. What was going on? I stood next to the piano staring at it.

Impetuously, I lifted the lid to discover an envelope with my name on it, wedged between the strings and the soundboard. My pulse shot through the ceiling. I tore open the envelope and read the first line:

My dearest Rory, by the time you read this, I will be dead...

# Post Script

*Los Angeles*
*Friday, May 12th 2017*
*1:30 p.m.*

I have never told anyone about the envelope I found wedged in the lyre of Marilyn's piano.

That was fifty-five years ago. Since then, my life has centered on my work as a journalist and author. I've been one of the lucky ones.

My career took a steady climb even though I refused to publish my experiences with the most iconic female film star to have ever filled the silver screen. She remains a fabled goddess who engages the attention of thousands of new fans yearly.

Having recently turned eighty, I've chosen this time to come forward to tell the adventure I lived through with Marilyn during the last few weeks of her life.

The interviews with the star have been sealed, and I am leaving them to the UCLA Department of Film and Cinematic Restoration, for publication, if and when they see fit after my passing. I could not bring myself to share these documents in my lifetime. The pain is still there after a half century.

I have just thanked the young lady who has spent many days taking down the dictation for this book, as my eyes can no longer focus on a keyboard for long periods of time. Oddly, she is twenty-five years old, the same age I was when I became involved with Marilyn. And she is also a journalism major. History is but an echo upon an echo.

As I began to tell the story of my time spent with Marilyn during the last two months of her life, I felt the need to reveal portions of the letter I found in the piano, which are not personal.

In very simple and straightforward language, she stated that she believed she was being stalked by several government agencies that utilize three capital letters to identify themselves. Weisman and I suspected there might have been another covert agency of which the public has no knowledge.

The circumstances surrounding her death remain a mystery.

Although I never got around to ask Marilyn about the details of her brief encounter with Elizabeth Short, the letter in the piano confirmed my suspicions. She had revealed the name of the doctor she feared to Marilyn. The name coincided with my research.

I have Marilyn to thank for information that led to a Pulitzer Prize for my book on the Black Dahlia.

Although my mother Rose lived to see the day I received the coveted award, unfortunately, my dear friend and mentor, Allan Weisman, had passed away. I dedicated it to him at the time. He taught me how to become what I became.

Carol Thompson and I had lunch after I received the prize. We relived our days at the paper, managing to find some laughs amongst all the sorrow that surrounded us.

Each day, I awaken with the image of Marilyn standing before me. This routine began the morning after she was found lifeless and alone.

Although much time has passed and my career as a writer has made complex demands upon my life, I have remained a creature of simple habits.

My desk sits beneath a large bay window that faces the garden of my Laurel Canyon bungalow. The sun crosses it every afternoon at different degrees depending upon the season. For a few minutes, light travels along my desktop.

When this occurs, I open a small box and place its contents on the desk.

I watch as the sun's rays create a rainbow of color reflected off a miniature typewriter fashioned from diamonds, gifted to me by a princess in a fairytale that took place once upon a time.

Rory Daniel Long
Los Angeles, California
2017

# Acknowledgements

Thanks go to F.J. Dagg, for his valuable commentary, to my wife Patricia for her constant support, and to Dr. Kenneth Atchity for his advice and encouragement along the long road home.

# About the Author

Art Johnson was born in San Diego, California in 1945. He contracted Polio Paralysis in 1950. Undaunted by the physical restriction, he became a musician, and moved to Hollywood in 1968. As a studio and touring professional he has recorded and performed with artists such as Lena Horne, Barbra Streisand and Luciano Pavarotti. He is a Grammy and Academy Award winning participant for music. As a solo recording artist with eight CDs to his credit, he is the executive consultant for a prominent jazz record label in the U.S. He began writing in the 1980's while working at The Philosophical Research Society in Los Angeles as one of several assistants to Manly Palmer Hall. He lectured at the Society for four years on the subjects of Humanities and the Arts focusing on poetry and poets. In 1990 Art returned to San Diego to become an adjunct faculty member of the San Diego Symphony. He holds an MA for music and was formerly a professor of improvisational studies at San Diego State University before moving to France in 2003. He currently resides in Monaco with his wife Patricia, where he continues to record and write.